The House that Marthasville Built

Nathan's Love Song

by Justin Hood

Table of Contents

Chapter 1   5

Chapter 2   21

Chapter 3   31

Chapter 4   41

Chapter 5   85

Chapter 6   113

Chapter 7   125

Chapter 8   139

Chapter 9   173

Chapter 10   191

Chapter 11   197

Chapter 12   239

Chapter 13   257

Chapter 14   293

Chapter 15   309

Chapter 16   333

Chapter 17   345

Chapter 18   373

Chapter 19   389

Chapter 20   395

Chapter 21   409

Chapter 1

After the Civil War, the small developing town Elijah Washington called home was only occupied by about 20 people. He was on the outskirts of town building the beginnings of a church.

There are many accounts in the Bible where God sees his people through the worst of times. Daniel was fed to the lions and came out without a scratch. Noah was placed in the worst rains the world had ever seen, but his faith in God is what saved his life. Even Jesus was put in places with people that were waiting to kill him, yet he stood fast in order to fulfill God's will. There are only two kinds of people that have faced death and survived, Christians and the Negro. I was born not too far from here about 35 years ago to a mother and father who were slaves. But the men in my family have always been men of the Lord, having prayer meetings and such in the woods late at night, giving people something to believe in despite what was going on around us. The masters didn't like us doing that back then, but we needed Jesus just as much as anybody.

They used to say, "if we catch any of you niggers disgracing our bible, we will punish you." I always found that amusing, that it was a sin for us to even want to know Jesus. Well, we never listened to that, so since we can preach now, I'm going to build my own church here in Marthasville. It's a small town with not a lot of people, but it's moving along nicely. We got people moving in every year or so and people having kids, so they need Jesus. I just hope that I can give him to them the right way. Just as Elijah finishes his thought, a man walks up behind him trying to get his attention. He is a tall, physically strong man with a dark complexion. He seems lost and not sure of where he actually is. He finally speaks up.

"Hello," says Walter. Shocked, Elijah says, "you scared the mess out of me boy now! I thought I was going to see the Lord a little sooner than I thought, and I have so much to do." They share a laugh.

"Now what can I help you with my friend," asked Elijah.

"I'm looking for Marthasville," Walter replied.

"Well, my friend, it looks like you found it. Names Elijah Washington, I'm the pastor here in town, you got business here in town, friend?"

"A little, if this map is correct, I own that piece of land over there." Walter points to a very nice plot of land not too far from where they were standing. It has a 'sold' sign on it with a small shack in the far corner. "Looks like I got some work to do."

"Brother, I think in some way we all do here in Marthasville. Say, I tell you what, if you help me every once in a while with this here church, I'll help you with your house," said Elijah. "Why you wanna help me, mister?" Walter asked.

"I don't know, I figure since we gone be neighbors we might as well help each other. It's still daylight outside, and we could get things done before nightfall. You still gone have to sleep in that shack, but at least it won't have chickens in it."

"No other reason?"

"Yea, there is another reason. A more important reason."

"Why?"

Elijah looks Walter in the face square and says to him, "Because I think God wants me to."

-

About 40 miles away at the state capital, a Congressional meeting is being held in a room filled with men from other parts of the state and country. They are all listening to the man standing at the podium giving a speech. He is a tall man with a slim build. He is white with brown eyes and a sharp nose and strong chin. He stands very well and talks properly with ease. Well dressed and has the attention of the entire room. "...With the changes that have been made since the war, we are forced into poverty. No more will the Negro have to work for nothing because he is owned by his master. They have stripped away our source of income to make the south weak so that they can

8

control the country. Lincoln says that they are entitled to a free way of life just like you and I well I say different. I say that the nigger does not deserve a chance to live his life as a free man because he wouldn't know how. I want to thank you all for voting me into this room because I promise you that I will make a difference. And contrary to what our beloved President has to say, I, Jeremiah Lesure, will make sure the south goes back to its way of life," concludes Mr. Lesure.

The entire room erupts into applause, and the men behind Mr. Lesure nod their heads in approval, as he waves to the people and thanks them for their vote.

After days of travel Mr. and Mrs. Lesure walk into their home after returning from the capital later on that evening.

Mrs. Lesure is a very pretty woman with red hair and green eyes. She is taller for a woman and outspoken. They live in an amazing mansion full of life and servants; mostly being black former slaves. They are walking through their home unwinding as they have a conversation.

"Did you hear the crowd react like that when you talked about a new south and how we will rise beyond the days of the civil war? It was what congress needed to hear after the last couple of years being forced to let our slaves go," said Mrs. Lesure.

"Yes, my love, it is time to reclaim the south and put ourselves back in this economic race. The Yankees's knew that if they took away our slaves, it would stop our most profitable way of income thus shutting us down and forcing us to live like them. The nigger has been a part of the south as much as cotton itself. And it is our right as American citizens to be able to own, sale and do what we wish with the niggers that we own."

"Do you ever think that there will be a day when the south will be what it was?"

"Well, my dear, if we stay on course with the majority of the vote going that way I don't see why not." Mr. Lesure walks over to Mrs. Lesure after getting comfortable in their house and hugs her passionately. "I want to thank you for all that you are doing for me to get me in that top seat."

"It's not a problem, my love."

Mr. Lesure cuts her off. "No, without the support of you and your family I would have never been in the position to be heard and applauded by Congress. Before I was just a writer at the local newspaper trying to relight the fire of the people in this state. And now I am close to being a very important person, and I have only you to thank." Mr. Lesure leans in to kiss his wife. But before it gets too intimate, she stops the kissing and remembers the beginnings.

"I remember reading your article in the paper every week when the paper was delivered to us. I would wait the whole week so that when I was done reading your pages, I wouldn't have to wait long to have the next one. Just having that paper in the house and having conversations with my daddy about being proud to be a white man in this country were some of the best times in my life. I can remember him telling us stories about the old south and how things use to be, and him saying that you were going to be someone of importance one day because you spoke what was on everyone's tongues. I can remember the first time I laid eyes on you in that small shop where they printed the newspaper. For some reason, I thought you would have been at least seven foot tall. You were every bit of handsome as I could have imagined, though, and from that point on I knew that you would be the one I would marry."

"Well, I'm grateful that you even gave me a chance. I remember that same day watching you walk into the newspaper office. When my boss told me that you were looking for me, I wondered if I owed you something or if you were someone that didn't like what I was saying. But I knew after that first visit that you were there for me and not what I was writing."
"How did you know?"

"Because the whole time we talked you never took your eyes off of me."

Mr. Lesure leans in for a kiss from his wife, but she pulls away and says, "Now, mister, you better stop trying to get fresh and worry about our guests that are about to come by. We have some very important people coming over for dinner, and we need to get ready before they start arriving. Lord knows I need to go down and check on the food and things. Can't leave that all up to the niggers now can we?"

12

Mrs. Lesure walks off with a look of concern while Mr. Lesure is none the wiser and thinks his wife is just being proactive as he goes to take a bath. It is a very big home with lots of paintings and vases typical for a wealthy and influential family of the time-to-have. Later on that evening in the middle of the dinner party Mr. and Mrs. Lesure are holding in their home, Mr. Lesure is talking among the men in the room who seem to be of importance. He has them all by the ear as he finishes his sentence. "So that is why I had to fire old Timothy. After so many days without a blacksmith, I thought I could just do it myself."

"Well, I sure do feel sorry for those horses," said one man.

"Why is that, Sir?"

"It's just sad that they will live out their natural lives uneven. They probably will think they were born that way." The men in the circle of conversation laugh and start to walk away as they pat Mr. Lesure on the back congratulating him on his position in congress and the speech that he had given. Everyone walks away to a different part of the party. Everyone except the man he was talking to from the beginning.

The man sticks his right hand out and says, "I want to thank you for having my family and I here at your home."

"You are more than welcome, thank you for coming, and I hope that you can come back in a month when my wife throws her annual gala. This year it will also be a masquerade ball."

"I look forward to the invitation. And I want to do something for you as well, in the morning I will be sending my blacksmith over to help with that shoeing of your horses. He is a young man, but he is very skilled at what he does."

"I don't know. Timothy as much of a misfit that he is, he was the fastest I know at shoeing a horse. The last time I believe he did it in two hours."

"That's good, but my boy can do it in one hour."

"That's unheard of."

"And that is why I am sending him to you first thing in the morning."

"My good man you are full of surprises. Is there anything else I should know about your blacksmith? Does he summon power from the earth and tame any animal of the wild with just a whisper as well?"

"If he does I would not be surprised. Oh, there is one other thing I think I should mention…"

"And what might that be?"

"He is a nigger, but he is good, and he works for nigger wages. And I promise that he will do a good job of it. Now, where is that lovely wife of yours? It's getting late, and I want to thank her for her hospitality this evening."

"Yes, of course. Let me find her." Mr. Lesure pulls one of the older servers close to him in a whisper and says, "Have you seen Mrs. Lesure around lately? Some of the guests are leaving and would like to say goodnight."

"Yes, Sir. I think I saw her and Ms. Catherine walk into the study some time ago. They must have gone in there to have some quiet from all the noise out here in the dining room."

"Yes, they must have."

The server rushes off back to her duties as if to not give time to say something that she shouldn't. Mr. Lesure looks at the study door to find that it is closed. "Would you go up to the study and have Mrs. Lesure come down for me?"

"Yes, Sir." The server hurries herself up the stairs to the study where Mrs. Lesure is. On the other side of the door, Mrs. Lesure and her friend lady Catherine are engaged in a passionate kiss trying their hardest not to get too excited. Catherine is a lot bolder than Mrs. Lesure is with her sexuality, chasing after Mrs. Lesure even when she tries to pull away.

"My, isn't it getting a little warm in here?"

"Yes, just the way we like it."

"Yes, but this isn't at your home or…"

"During the day while your husband is at work? Or in the horse stables during the night with nothing but the light from the lantern to help me see where to touch you?"

"Yes, this is not the time, nor the place for us to be inappropriate."

Catherine continued chasing Mrs. Lesure around the room trying to be seductive and trying to convince Mrs. Lesure of what she wants. Mrs. Lesure is only telling her no because of where they are. It is obvious that they are involved in a relationship. "Well, I don't feel like I am being inappropriate at all."

"Are you mad? Do you not know what will happen to the two of us if we were ever caught in such a manner? We will be sent away to asylums where I have heard they force men on you to fix you."

"I don't care. I love you, Mary, and I don't mind people knowing that I have and always will."

"Well, as much as I love you too I cannot and will not let you tear everything that I have worked for, down. After this whole mess is worked out in congress about the niggers being free, I will then work on my husband to help with women's rights. Then when that is done, we will be..."

"Are you going to leave him?"
"No, why would I do such a thing?"

"Because you don't love him, and because whenever I get close to you, it's as if you are fighting something that you and I know is boiling inside of you." Catherine goes to give Mrs. Lesure a soft kiss. They kiss, and then there is a knock at the door.

"Mrs. Lesure?! Mr. Lesure is down at the party and is asking for your presence. Some of

the guests are leaving and would like to say goodnight." The server heads back down the
stairs. She never opens the door. Most of the help knows about the affair Mrs. Lesure is
having with Catherine.

"Okay, we will be right down."

"Are you going to see me after all of this is over and done? Or will I be waiting months to see you because you have to make sure your husband stays on track?" "I will see you when the time is right for the both of us."

"It's not me that isn't making the time, it's you. Maybe one day when you decide to face the person that you are you will see me." Catherine walks out of the room as Mrs. Lesure goes to fix her clothes. Her face shows that she is worried about losing control of the situation with Catherine. Mrs. Lesure stands there for a moment only to reflect on the history of Catherine and her relationship.

Chapter 2

Mrs. Lesure had joined some other women for an afternoon of tea so they could catch up on the daily events. The group of ladies was in a deep discussion about the freedom of the woman of the times.

"So that is why I believe that one day we will be treated equal to men and not just be used for cleaning, running a house and having children." The room lights up with applause and joy as the other ladies in the room take in what Mrs. Lesure is saying about the future. One lady chimes in.

"Well, I think that cleaning and child rearing is part of what makes us women. I mean the bible says that we should be that for our households, so why is being a housewife such a bad thing?"

"It's not, all we are saying is that in addition to what we do around the house we can do so much more. For our husbands and for ourselves as well, take Milly Bloomberg for example. Now just three years ago they were the richest and most revered family in the land. Mr. Bloomberg rest his soul dies in a horse riding accident, and now Milly is barely keeping her house together because he never took the time to show her the basics of running the home. The bills, who and what is and isn't paid, so that when these men try to get extra money out of us, we know better. And it's not because we want to be them or take their place at the head of the household, it's to strengthen the family so that in case of any situation the family will continue to strive."

The women in the room begin to applaud Mrs. Lesure. The ladies begin to file out of the room as if the meeting was over and one-by-one say good evening to Mrs. Lesure and comment on her speech of the evening. A younger looking Catherine walks up to Mrs. Lesure and starts to speak to her.

"I have never heard a woman talk with such confidence before. I have heard great things about you, and what you are trying to do and I am glad to say that as of tonight I believe every single word."

"Why thank you, Ms.?"

"Catherine Anderson."

"Aw, from the Andersons of Kellyville, I'm guessing."

"You guessed well."

"I hear you have a wonderful plantation out there."

"Thank you. You know there was one thing that they didn't tell me about you."

"And what was that?"

"How absolutely breathtaking you are."

There is an older woman listening to the conversation, and she is taken aback by what she has just heard. She gives the expression as if she is not sure if Catherine just tried to hit on Mrs. Lesure.

"Well...Thank you for that lovely compliment. I hope that my husband to be will feel the same way."

"Well, I hope he will as well."

They shake hands as to say goodnight to each other. The touch of Catherine to Mrs. Lesure's, shows a connection between the two. Catherine in her look is certain about the feeling, whereas Mrs. Lesure is left to feel an unease. She quickly retracts her hand from Catherine and says her goodbye's for the night. Flashback to the present, where Mr. and Mrs. Lesure are standing at their front door saying goodbye to the guests of the evening. One-by-one they say their peace before they leave, until Catherine walks up. Mrs. Lesure is in almost a fearful state knowing what could come from Catherine's mouth. Catherine turns and says to the both of them, "Thank you once again for inviting me into your home and having such a wonderful dinner."

"You are always welcome to our home. You and my wife are great friends, and she holds you in high regard. It is our honor to have you here anytime that you decide." "Elizabeth, you better mind your husband. He keeps on treating me this way I might just have to steal him away. Good night to you both. I will be by later this week to visit if that is okay?"

"As a matter of fact, I have to leave for the capital in a couple of days and was wondering if you would maybe stay a while to keep my wife company. I know you have your own plantation to take care of, but it would be a favor to me if my wife could have your company for if only a moment."

"Well, I can move some things around and come back in a couple of days."

"Great, I will have the servants prepare the guest room for your return."

"Okay, well I will be returning then. I will see you in a couple of days, Elizabeth."

Catherine leaves the house and gets into her carriage ride while Mr. and Mrs. Lesure watch the carriage leave.

Mr. Lesure turns to his wife and says, "You know, Catherine really enjoys you."

"What do you mean?"

"She seems to care a lot about you and wants to see you happy. If I am not careful, she may try to take you away from me."

Mrs. Lesure looks at her husband with an unsure look as if he knows or not that she is involved with Catherine. She also is concerned about Catherine's return to the house knowing what will happen.

Will she fight the temptations and advances Catherine will make or will she give into the woman that she has fallen in love with?

-

Walter and Elijah were sitting outside cooking a piece of meat over their campfire. The food is just about done when Elijah begins speaking "So I haven't asked you, where are you from?"

"I was born in Tennessee. I joined the Union Army about two years ago when they finally decided to let niggers fight and ended up in Texas. I saved up the little money that they gave us to finally buy my own land, which is right over there."

"Got any family?"

"No."

"You surely have someone in your family?"

"No, my mother and father were sold to a family in Louisiana some years back. Haven't seen nor heard from them since. What about you, preacher? Where do you come from?" "I'm from a small town not too far from here. My daddy picked cotton, and my mother was a house cook. But at night back in the woods, my father would hold prayer meetings to uplift the people from what we had to deal with every day. Beatings, and having to work for nothing for long hours in a day, hell the only thing we had sometimes was God. My father was a good man, that is until—" There was a small pause and silence in the air. Walter looks over at Elijah who is reliving what he is saying in his mind, "...until they killed him for preaching. It's funny how white people read the bible to you. Telling you that it is God's command for us as nigger's to be the property of the white man. But if we ever wanted to believe in God or read about him ourselves, that it was a sin punishable by death. One day they found my father and two other preachers like him trying to read a bible that was left to them by some traveling Christians from the north. They beat my father until he couldn't say his own name and burned him to show us that we should never do it again."

"So why did you become a preacher yourself?"

"Because it was the last thing my Pa asked me to do. He said, "Son, you have always had the Spirit.""

"When I was a young boy, I drowned in the lake close to my house. The master's son thought that it would be fun to see how long a nigger child could hold his breath. So he dragged me down to the lake and held me under until I couldn't breathe anymore. When they found me I was dead. Some say for at least an hour before Pa began to pray out loud and all of a sudden I was alive. I remember hearing his prayers bringing me back to life. From then on my Pa said that I had a special gift and that I could only use it for the Lord."

"And you believe it?"

"Yes."

"Why?"

"Because through all the things that have happened in my life, I know one thing is for sure, and that is God is real. And if he wanted me to be a preacher then that is what I was going to do."

"Seems a little weird to me."

"Well, if believing in someone greater than you is weird, then I am one weird fella. Sometimes, you just gotta go on faith. Cause a lot of times it's the only thing left. Now, since I cooked for you this evening I hope that you will help me clean up."

"Of course, it's what God would have wanted." They both share a laugh and start to clean up the area.

Chapter 3

On the other side of town at a share cropping station, there are three Negro men trying to collect their wages for a job that they have completed. The person before them is a white man who only has done half of the job the three Negroes have done, he steps up and gets his cotton weighed for sale. The man turns to him and says,"Well, Henry you did some mighty fine work today. You worked real hard. So I am going to give you twenty-five cents a pound. You picked nine pounds today, so that brings your wages to two dollars and cents. Are you coming back tomorrow, Henry?"

"Yes, Sir. You men treat me so fair I wouldn't have it any other way."

"Good. We will see you bright and early in the morning."

"Okay. See you in the morning, Jim."

The three Negroes are next in line to receive their wages for the job that they have done. The Negro has at least eighteen pounds of cotton ready to be weighed. You can tell by the look on his face that he knows he should be getting a pretty penny for the work he and his sons have done.

"Hey there, Mr. Jim, how are you this evening?"

"I'm good, John. Just wrapping things up here so that I can get home for supper. The Mrs. made apple pie this afternoon, and I cannot wait to sink my teeth into a slice."

"I'm sure she has made a pie to die for, I won't take up more time then I have to then because I know you are trying to get home. Me and the boys did some really good work out there, so I hope we don't break you any." As John finishes his sentence, Jim looks up at the scale and sees that there are eighteen pounds of cotton on the scale. At least nine more pounds of cotton than the man before.

"Okay, John I see that you and your boys have picked eighteen pounds of cotton today at ten cents a piece, which brings you to one dollar and eight cents."

One of the twins is getting tired of always being cheated by the men that weight out the cotton. As his father tries to understand why they would be making so little for doing the bulk of the work, his son finally says something. "Well, you see Mr. Jim we brought you at least nine more pounds of cotton than Mr. Henry did, and you gave him 25 cents a pound. I reckon that at that rate I would be getting about five dollars."

"Well, that would be the case, but it's three of you. I can't pay all three of you at the same rate, now can I?"

'Well, I guess not."

John's son, Matthew, interrupts the conversations between Jim and his father. "Well, if that is the case then split the pounds into threes. We did equal work, so it looks like you owe us a dollar and seventy-five cents a piece." The father and twin son Mark looks at each other in disbelief as well as the sharecropping station employees. Mr. Jim spits on the ground and walks over to Matthew to ask him a couple of questions.

"Is that right boy? Then tell me, have you ever run a cropping station before?"

"No, Sir."

"So how do you know what I should be paying my employees? Especially some niggers who less than ten years ago would get nothing but a chicken and somewhere to sleep."

"Well, good thing this isn't ten years ago."

"What you say, boy?"

"Nothing, Mr. Jim. He must be tired from all of this heat lately."

"Yea, I guess the heat must be messing with him."

"Yes, Sir. So at ten cents a pound, we should be at one dollar, and eighty cents is that correct, Mr. Jim?" Mr. Jim counts out the wages for the day and gives it to Matthew and says, "Your brother needs to mind his manners heat or no heat."

"I understand. Sir. Me and Pa will have a talking to him when we get home."

"You do that."

Mr. Jim looks at Mark and says, "Mark I think you need to take a lesson from your brother here in manners. It'd be a shame you come up missing like those boys a while back."
"You right Mr. Jim, it would be a shame if I came up missing. And as far as my brother, we are more alike than you may think, Mr. Jim. But thank you for your opinion on it." Mr. Jim looks at the other men behind him and chuckles because he knows he got his way and point across. "You're welcome. Will we see you and your family in the morning?"

"Yes Sir, Mr. Jim. We will see you first thing," Matthew said as he walked away. John is furious and somewhat puzzled by Mark's actions. As they walk away from the plantation, John grabs his son by the shirt and throws him to the ground.

35

"What has come over you, boy! Your mother is probably sick in her grave wondering what the hell has come over you! Ever since your uncle was hung three years ago, you act like white people won't string you up! They have always done good by us as a family, and I have always taught you to respect them because without them we would be dead! Now, this is the last time I will be telling you anything about something like this or so help me God I will kill you myself!"

John walks away and makes the hand movements as if he is praying about the situation. Matthew watches his father walk away and then is helped up by his brother, who is somewhat laughing.

"What's so funny? "You almost getting us killed?" Matthew raised his voice in a mocking manner, "*Mr. Jim, me and my brother are more alike than you know.* Do you know what would have happened if I wouldn't have stepped in?"

"That's the point, Matt. Uncle did not take all that time teaching us our native way of fighting just so we can be cowards every time the white man pokes his chest out."

36

"And what did that get our beloved Uncle, Mark? Huh? It got him hung when they found out that it was him who beat up Mr. Jim's nephew."

"He deserved it! He stole one of our pigs and said it was his. And when the courts found us guilty and made us pay a fine to him because of it, Uncle took matters into his own hands."

"And where is he now? Huh? In the ground, for the last three years, that's where he is. And you know what he told me before he died? He said don't be stupid! Be smart enough to know when and where to pick your battles. We gotta keep fighting them their way, through the courts! It's the only way we will win!" "Is that so?" Mark asked.

"That's so," said Matthew.

'Then what we will be doing later on tomorrow night is through the courts?"

Matthew looks at Mark with a blank stare knowing what he is talking about. Mark gets as close as a whisper to his brother and says. "I know you are trying to do things by the book. And one day that might work, but for now there will be a time when we will have to break a couple of rules. Now, I will ask you right now, right here before we get any further with our missions. I have been with you doing this for a year and a half now. How can you question my loyalty to the cause?"

"Because of your great planning we have yet to be seen, but what is going to happen when they wise up? You know, one thing I have learned about people is that we are all smart. No matter what race, so the things that we are getting away with by planning will soon be figured out. Then what are you going to do? Are you going to talk your way out of it when they find out what we have been doing?"

"Then and only then will I defend myself, but only to escape, never because I have too much pride. Now you can say all you want, but you know as well as I, that if anything was to happen out there, I am the one and only person you can count on. Always have been, always will be."

"You being there for me is not what I worry about."

"Then what do you worry about?"

"You being there for yourself if the time ever comes."

Mark walks away from his brother down the road as Matthew watches him. He starts walking in the opposite way of their home. Matthew says, "Hey, where are you going?"

"Down to Mrs. Debbie's!"

"But supper is in an hour!"

"Then that's when I will be home!"

Chapter 4

Mark enters a small bar owned by a very large woman by the name of Debbie.

Debbie hugs Mark as he walks into the room.

"Hey, Stranger! It's been a while since you been in. Where have you been?"

"Working with Matthew and Pa in the cotton fields."

"When the fellas said that you would be here tonight I didn't believe it not one bit. I said Mrs. Debbie the money that boy made in here last time there was no way you would be returning here. Now, what brings you back into Mrs. Debbie's?"

"Need to make a little bit more money to help me finish something I started."

"Okay, well the boys are out back and they been drinking waiting on you. The fella they brought is a very big man, so you be careful as always."

Debbie kisses Mark on the head and says, "Good luck, sugar."

"Thanks, Mrs. Debbie. Mrs. Debb?"

"Yes, honey?"

"Do you kiss those guys on the head before fights like you do me?"

"Heavens no. I just warn them."

Mark smiles at Mrs. Debbie, and she smiles back. "Now gone back there and make some money."

"I won't be long," Mark said.

"You never do."

Mark walks quickly to the back of the bar and catches the eye of a young man sitting at a table writing something. He looks at Mark and quickly goes back to his work. Mrs. Debbie looks over at him and shakes her head and says, "Boy, the way you keep writing on those pages you would think the white man was okay with you knowing how to spell. You better be glad white folks don't come this way looking for nothing or you would have been strung up by now."

"That's what makes you so special, Mrs. Debbie. Why them white folks ain't never close you down like them other spots we use to have," said Nathan.
"It's because Debbie always has a plan for a plan. My daddy taught me that years ago."

"And what's that supposed to mean?"

"It means that you need to put up that paper and get on that piano and get to playing before I take you out front and string you up myself."

Nathan walks up to the piano and gets situated by moving little small things around to make himself comfortable. He puts a couple of pages of music notes onto the piano and pauses, gets up and goes out to the back of the bar where Mark is located.

At the same time, Mark is walking into the back of the bar talking smack to the other men standing there waiting on him. One older man stands and watches Mark waiting on him to be ready as he has brought a massive man with him to fight Mark. Bubba is at least six and a half feet and at least 300 pounds. He's bald and missing his front teeth, but has gold replacements. He wears no shirt, but has on overalls and shoes that look like they have been worked. Bubba laughs at the size of Mark as he walks into the room and then his trainer says, "I see you finally showing up boy! You sure you don't wanna have a drink before you lose this fight?" asked the man.

"No, I think I will pass on the drink and what makes you so sure this time you will win?" replied Mark.

"This is Bubba! He is a field hand that... let's say can do more than most. Why I witnessed this man pick up at least four or five bails of tobacco by himself. You know he once even pulled an entire stagecoach that had a broken down horse into town about three miles out. Son, I think tonight you will have your hands full."

"Well, tell Bubba there that he may have his hands full with me. I'm glad you guys gave me a chance to get ready, and once the music starts, I will be ready to go."

There is no music in the air yet, and Mark wonders what Nathan is doing. "Like I said once the music starts I will be ready to go!"

As Mark says it again Nathan opens the door and says, "What song was that you wanted to hear again?"

"I don't remember! It was the song you played last time I was here. It had an upbeat to it, really gets the party going," said Mark.

"You mean the one that I played from Mozart or the one I wrote?"

"I don't know! Look, you making me look bad right now in front of the fellas right now." says Mark. "So what you want me to do?" Nathan asked. "Just play what you feel, Nathan."

He mumbled under his breath, "Why is it so hard to find people to do the simplest things around here? I ask for the same song every time I come in here and every time I have to whoop ass to a different tune."

Nathan starts to play the song, and the fight starts. Mark notices that he is playing a basic song like chopsticks and begins to laugh. Mark starts off fighting in an early English boxing stance that the men in the room find funny to see. Bubba swings at Mark with all of his might and misses as Mark dodges the blow and pushes him in the back. Bubba tries again only to be treated the same way but this time kicked in the ass for show. Bubba doesn't like the fun that Mark is having, so he grabs Mark while he is not looking and throws him into a small pile of potato sacks discarded in the corner of the room. The

46

men in the crowd grow more confident and begin to bet more money against Mark. Mark notices this and shows a small smile, he rolls out of the way of a foot from Bubba and gets back on his feet. At this time Nathan is starting to play a jazzed up form of chopsticks that Mark really likes and thus becomes a little lighter on his feet. Bubba becomes distracted because it is almost as if Mark is starting to dance to the music, he is not sure if he is still fighting.

"Are you going to fight or are you going to buy me a drink, boy," said Bubba.

"I tell you what, when I'm done working you over I'll buy you that drink cause you gone need it. Now come on big fella, Pa made supper, and he don't like me to be late," said Mark.

As Mark is finishing his sentence, Bubba rushes him and grabs him up. He starts to try to squeeze the life out of Mark as Mark starts to punch Bubba in the face. He lets Mark go, and he once again is angered by Mark's dancing while fighting style.

"This ain't no game boy, either you fight me or you're going to be dancing all the way to the doctor."

"Well, you bring your big ass over here so that I can show you how much of a dancer I am.
Bubba runs over to Mark and is met by a series of kicks to the stomach and face. Half of the crowd stands in amazement as the other half looks on as if they have seen this before and are upset that they have bet against Mark again.

At the same time outside there is a small horse and carriage riding in with a man and woman on the back. There are four more people riding separate horses but are close behind listening to the music the man and the woman on the carriage are playing. They seem to be trying to come up with lyrics to a song when the woman overhears the sound of the piano that Nathan is playing at Mrs. Debbie's. "Do you hear that," asked Carolyn.

"Hear what," a man asked.

"That music. It's coming from that small little building over there. I wanna see who that is playing."

"Cat, I heard that is a nigger town. They say it's the only nigger town anywhere in the south," another man said.

"Well, nigger town or no nigger town I want to see the face of the person playing that piano."

Nathan is really enjoying the music that he is making on the piano and starts to step the melody up into a jazz/funk sound, and Mark is in the back of the bar beating the sense out of Bubba, finally kicking him through the back doors and stumbling to a seat at the bar. Mark picks up his belongings and winnings and walks back into the bar. He tips Nathan for the song, Mrs. Debbie for the damages and buys Bubba his drink. He then walks out of the front door of the bar where Carolyn and her bandmate are standing and watching Nathan at the piano. She walks over to a table near the piano and takes a seat. Mrs. Debbie walks over to the table and asks, "Is there anything that I can help you with?"

"Sure, you got any whiskey around here?" Carolyn replied.

"Just got some in, this morning."

"Well, may I have a glass and whatever the man at the piano is having."

"Who, Nathan? That boy don't drink. He just come in here to play the piano. But if you really wanna get him something to drink, we got nice cold sodas in the back."

"In that case, bring him two."

Mrs. Debbie walks away puzzled as if she doesn't quite understand why this white lady out of nowhere wants to buy Nathan a drink. She knows for a fact that she doesn't want him as a man because of the way race mixing is dealt with in the south, or so she thinks. She quickly brings the bottle to Carolyn and walks over to Nathan and gives him the bottles of soda.

"This is from the lady at the table."

"What for?" Nathan asked.

"I don't know. But any white woman that will buy you a drink in this town you have to be real careful about, you know?"

"Yes, Ma'am."

Carolyn talks softly to Nathan from across the room only to get his attention, but not for him to understand her. Nathan gets up and walks over to the table Carolyn is sitting at. He sits across from her as to not invade her space and says, "I wanna thank you for buying me the soda, but I hope you don't mind me asking what for?"

"My name is Carolyn, and I am a part of a band over in the city. We been all over this country playing and I think this might be where I find my fame."

"Think so? Well, Miss, I hope you find what you are looking for."

"You know, I think I have. Say, you think you could show me how you were playing that piano? I heard you on the way in and I thought it was the most interesting way of playing chopsticks."

Nathan and Carolyn walk back toward the piano so that he can show her the tune. Mrs. Debbie is standing in the background shaking her head as if she has a feeling about the situation going on in her bar. She is almost nervous to have this strange woman in her bar where no white person would visit at that time of day. Also seeing that there are two men standing in the doorway. She has a short barrel shotgun under the bar that she glances at as she cleans her mason jars.

"Sure, it was the first song I ever learned how to play. There was a man that was just passing through that showed me how to play that before he left and from then on I just added to it as I learned the keys."

Nathan shows Carolyn the basic keys to the song and slowly adds to it as she looks on in amazement. She cannot believe that this black man is playing the piano so well. Outside, the rest of the band begins to listen and sneak peeks inside Ms. Debbie's to see Carolyn sitting next to Nathan. They pace back and forth in front of the bar as if they do not like the fact she is spending so much time with Nathan. Nathan finishes showing her how to play the song and says, "And that is what I like to call *Nathan's Chopsticks*."

"Well, I think that is an amazing version to know how to play. You are a talented kid, what is your name again?"

"Nathan, Ma'am. You know Nathan's Chopsticks."

"Got it. Well, Nathan Chopsticks it is a pleasure to have listened to you tonight, but I can see that my friends are becoming a little restless."

Nathan looks passed the piano to see the men standing at the door waiting for Carolyn to come out of the bar so that they can leave. He also notices that one man, in particular, seems to be a little more upset than the others, he is a shorter gentleman and bald with green eyes. Nathan asks Carolyn, "Why does he seem so upset?"

Carolyn gets up from the table and walk's toward the door and says, "Because he is our piano player; and also happens to be my husband."

Nathan watches Carolyn walk out the door only to finally meet the eyes of the bald gentleman at the door. He is furious at the fact that his wife is even talking to this man, let alone him being black. But he says nothing to her and directs all his anger toward Nathan and his ability to get Carolyn's attention. Carolyn gets into the wagon and looks back at the bar. She sees Mrs. Debbie and waves goodbye. Mrs. Debbie, however, gives a questionable wave and before they were out of site, she turns to go back into the bar to talk to Nathan.

"So what did she want with you?"

"She just asked me about my way of playing Chopsticks and how I learned to play the piano. Nothing too serious, why do you ask?"

"Because out of the ten years that I been serving liquor out this place, I have never seen a white woman around here. Let alone come and listen to some music."

"You think?"

"Honey, I have been in this small town since it started. And when I tell you white people don't come in this town unless they are looking for something or someone. I mean it."

"Yes, Ma'am."

"So do me a favor, Sugar. If that little lady comes around again asking questions about you and the way you play that there piano. Do yourself a favor and stay away, she won't bring you nothing but trouble."

"How do you know that?"

"White people always bring trouble to people they don't like. Hell, ask the Indians." Mrs. Debbie walks off of the stage that the piano and Nathan are sitting on and goes back to her bar. Nathan plays with the keys as he ponders his excitement about what Carolyn was saying and Mrs. Debbie's concerns about it.

Mark walks into his father's house for dinner. Matthew looks at his watch and back at his brother to show that it is a little later than he was expecting. Their father is coming back from the kitchen with the last of the food and asks Mark, "Where did you go after work, boy?"

"I went down to Mrs. Debbie's bar to have a beer before I came home. You know, think about some things before I got here."

"And.."

"And I wanted to say sorry for what I did this evening. I'm just tired of the white man taking advantage of us. I mean he gave Mr. Henry twice as much a pound of cotton as he did us and we did more! I just can't understand if we did more work how he came out with more money?"

"Well, Mr. Jim pays us what he wants! We should be thankful that they pay us in the first place! Son, I can remember a time when we worked that same field for little of nothing. So for Mr. Jim to give us anything is a blessing in itself."

Mark and Matthew look at each other in disbelief. They both have their views on white America. Mark being the fight for what is right type and Matthew believing that the government will correct itself. But the one thing that they both believe is that the white man will not solve any of the problems that the black man has or will have. Mark sits at the table with a lot to say but holds back because of the trouble he was in with his father. Matthew notices him holding back and chimes in and asks their father. "So Pa, why do you feel the white man is the answer," asked Matthew.

"Well, because they always have been. My father was one of the first of our family to be in this part of the country, and we have always been taken care of. He worked in the house in the kitchen as a cook, and my mother was a caregiver for Mr. Jim's family. Hell, she actually took care of Mr. Jim for most of his childhood."

"Is that why Mr. Jim takes the time out treat us so good?", says Mark.

Matthew chimes in to keep the peace between his father and brother as he kicks Mark under the table.

"What he means Pa is it's kind of hard to understand that if your parents took care of Mr. Jim when he was a little one, you would think he would treat us a little better because of it."

"Well, that is up to Mr. Jim and what his family has to deal with. It's more than just paying us for the work; cotton isn't as profitable as it once was."

"Yea, especially since now you have to pay the workers." Matthew and Mark get a laugh out of what was just said. John does not see the humor in it at all seeing that he actually lived it.

"Listen here, boys! There was a time where you couldn't even talk to white folks outright, let alone be paid anything from them. You either did it, or they lynched you, simple as that. There was no talking or convincing of anything, just what boss man wanted, and that was that. I remember a time where we had a man on the plantation that corrected Mr. Jim's father about how to plow a field in front of his friends. Later on that night Mr. Jim's father came to his house with a couple of his friends and hung him in the middle of our town. And to add to it, they made us leave him there for a week just so that we would know never to talk over him again. So coming from that to what we have now is a big step. The white man don't have to give us nothing at all!"

"That's the point I am trying to make, Pa. Why is it that we have to be given something? You know we are the only people of color that did not protest slavery? The Indians fought for their freedom. The Mexicans and the Asians."

"And look what that got them? Either dead or in jail doing what the white man wanted them to do anyway." said Pa.

"Yea, but there is a difference." replied Mark.

"And what is that, son?"

"They may have died or went to jail. But at least they still had their pride while doing it." Mark finishes his sentence and starts in on his dinner for the night. Matthew looks at his father as if Mark has a sound point but does not say anything to keep the conversation going. John thinks for a moment about what his son just said to him. Maybe he does have an old way of thinking, and his son may have a point. There is no other race in the history of America that did not violently fight for the right to be free, even the first Americans fought the British in order to call America their home.

Elijah and Walter are finishing up their work before the end of the night. Elijah has a small shack that he is living in while he is building a church and offers Walter a place to sleep. Elijah is making a bed for Walter on the floor of the shack next to his bed.

He throws some blankets down with a big cloud of smoke coming from the floor.

Walter finishes up the dish cleaning and says to Elijah, "Thanks for a place to sleep."

"No worries, my father always said the least you could do for a person in need is a hot meal and a place to rest."

"Tell me something, preacher. Why do you think the world is the way it is?"

"What do you mean, Walter?" asks Elijah.

"Well, when I was a young boy I thought that white and black people didn't get along. But as I grew up I see that it's more than that, not only do whites and blacks not get along, but most people of different races hate each other. Even poor white folks are treated badly by the rich ones."

"Well, honestly I blame Adam and Eve."

"Why them?"

"Whelp, the bible says that once Adam and Eve ate from the apple they noticed that they were naked. Most people think that once they did that they opened up their minds to the right of choice. What is right and what is wrong, but I think that what eating the apple did was gave them the ability to see the difference in people. You have to remember God had already given Adam choice by allowing him to name all the animals and things he saw. It's not until right after eating it they notice that they were naked, or saw the difference between man and woman. It's also how Cain saw that Able seems to be favored by God, which is why he killed him."

"So you're saying that the one thing Adam and Eve gained in eating the apple was difference?"

"When you meet new people in your life, one of the first things that you do is start to size them up. See if you're bigger, smarter or faster than the person. Those are the feelings that always grow into hate, young man."

Walter shakes his head in agreement with what Elijah is saying. Maybe the world's hate comes from our mistakes even before we knew of them. Most people that read the bible never take the time out to see it for what it actually is. It's a book written by the prophets of God in their view of what was going on at the time.

Elijah and Walter lay in their beds looking at the night sky through a hole in the ceiling. Walter looks into the sky at the stars for a moment and then says to Elijah.

"I suppose I should be finding the supply store around here so that I can get to work on my land, maybe order some wood for the house. So by the time it gets here I can be ready to build. Plant a couple of things, you think maybe you could show me around, preacher?" "Sure! It'd be my pleasure. We can go, and I'll introduce you to Kimberly, she runs the store for Mr. Wiliams out here, so he not down here much. A very attractive woman too, her father was black, and her mother was Indian who almost passes for white. Every man for miles around have come here to have her hand in marriage, but she will have none of it, no sir, she says.

 "Well, she hasn't met me yet, so at least there is a little hope." says Walter.

"Who, you? You wouldn't stand a chance."

"And what makes you think so, preacher?"

"You too ugly, yea you might have a little land and a couple of dollars but Kimberly wouldn't be caught dead with a face like that by her side."

Walter laughs to himself as Elijah is talking. Walter is serious in his concern for Kimberly, it's not that he is interested in her as a mate but more as a great friend.

"Well, I guess I won't be putting too much thought into Kimberly. I wouldn't want to insult her or anything like that."

"Now you are making sense."

"Goodnight, preacher man."

"Goodnight, Walter"

They both stargaze and wonder about the future and what it holds for the both of them. Elijah can tell that Walter is not telling him everything that is going on in his life, which is okay because Elijah has some demons that he has not revealed to the world as well. We are all imperfect in a way, no one is following God's commandments by the book, but we all try to the best of our abilities. We put a lot of pressure on ourselves as a People to seem perfect, but because of the original sin, I don't think that was God's intent. He knows that we will never be perfect, he just wants us to try to at least follow the perfect footsteps of his son.

Carolyn and her band are in the local white bar and concert hall playing their music for the people that attended the party they were hired for. Carolyn is concerned because she can tell that the crowd is not appreciating the music. They seem somewhat bored by the melodies that they are playing. Carolyn is next to go on and stands next to the owner of the club at the ready. The owner is not pleased by the reaction of the crowd. He turns to Carolyn and says, "This isn't turning out like what you said in your letters," said the club owner.

"It's only the first night. Give us a chance," replied Carolyn.
"To what, learn how to play the music? Your band is horrible! Where did you find these guys?"

"They aren't that bad."

"Your trumpet player plays as if he just got the thing, your drummer is okay, but if no one else can play the music, it doesn't matter. And the piano player needs to be taken out to pasture and shot! What made you bring him with you anyway?"

"He is my husband."

"Makes sense because that is the only way he could have made it on the wagon!" Carolyn pauses for a minute and says to the owner, "Give me five more minutes to prove to you that we should be here."

"I will give you five minutes, after that you and your friends will be out on the street, and there won't be a place within 400 miles that will hire you."

Carolyn walks away from the club owner knowing that she doesn't have anything that will help the situation. She walks up on stage and stops the band, she starts to talk to them about the next song that they are going to try to play for the crowd, but as she scans them, she notices the people are not happy with what has gone on so far. There are people that are walking out, finishing their drinks and headed to the Saloon across the road. She can hear the celebrations that are going on in the nearby Saloon and also notices that other people are starting to follow the first couple that left to go across the road. She has a look of defeat on her face, and at the same time, her husband grabs her hand to pull her off the stage as if their chance is over and then Carolyn has an idea.

"Ladies and Gents I know that we haven't been the band you wanted to hear this evening. My piano player isn't feeling the best, but I think I have something that will get this thing going. So order another round of drinks, and I promise by the morning you will be telling those folks that walked out of here that they missed the best band this town has ever seen."

Carolyn looks back at the crowd and notices that she doesn't have the ear of the ladies in the room, but the men in the room are willing to give her a chance. She doesn't want to leave their fate to chance, so she goes over to the piano and replaces her husband. She slides him nicely off of the piano with a kiss and a smile that he enjoys but at the same time as he walks off infuriates him. She begins to play slowly to get the hang of Nathan's Chopsticks, as she starts to play the crowd laughs at it because it is a basic song that they all know from their childhood. At that point of laughter, she starts to pick up the melody of the song as Nathan had shown her just hours before their show. She starts to get into the song, and the crowd loves it, they start to dance and order more drinks as Carolyn adds to the tune she was taught. The people love it, and the ones that have left are starting to return and enjoy the music as the club owner stands and shakes his head in approval. Carolyn keeps playing the song and also notices the disapproval of it from her husband.

Carolyn gets paid by the owner, who tells her good night for the evening. She walks up the stairs into the room that they have rented to stay the night and her husband is furious. He slams the door behind her and says, "What in the hell were you thinking?!"

"What I was thinking is why in the world would I let us lose a well paying job because we can't find things to play? Why is it that I have to travel with this man from town-to-town trying to find a job with a band that can't play instruments? Or the bigger question is why do I stay with a man that can't play basic keys on a piano, but claims to be a piano player?"

Her husband becomes angry for hearing what she has said to him. He pushes her against the wall, and before he can hit her, she says, "Go ahead and hit me! That way if you hurt me or break something we can go back to stealing and living off the land! Maybe one day if we are lucky we can try to rob a bank because we are THAT poor and they will hang us!"

"Who are you talking to like this?"

"The man that is standing in front of me! The man that I have trusted with my life and heart for the last five years, that promised me the world and instead has given me nothing but hurt and a taste for beef jerky! Well, I'm tired of jerky, I want the steaks and the pretty dresses that you promised me I would have if I stayed with you. And I have, through thick and thin stayed with you despite living off the land and not getting those dresses that I so want. So I did what I had to do so that we wouldn't have to keep moving all over the country for nothing. I want a home."

"I understand all of that, but to play a song written by a nigger?!"

"Do you know how much money we just made for that "nigger" song? We just made fifty dollars in one night for playing a song that we didn't come up with. That nigger will never be able to come in this Saloon and play his music but we sure can, and if it's going to bring us all those things that we have been praying for then so be it, what's it to a nigger who would never be able to perform them anyway."

Carolyn's husband stands there in thought. He understands what Carolyn is saying but doesn't totally believe what she is saying about Nathan. Yes, he understands that the boy would never be able to perform his songs for a white crowd. And he understands the fact that they could make a lot of money using his songs as a base for the new material they need to come up with in order to stay in town. But deep down he fears that there is more to Carolyn and Nathan then she is letting on. He looks at her in her eyes as if he is trying to pull the truth out of her as Carolyn looks back and says nothing waiting on his answer.

71

"You make sure that is the only thing you are doing with that nigger across the river. You know what happened to the last one I thought was giving you the eye."

"Yes, I know. You and your friends made me watch as you strung him to that tree. Despite the fact that I told you he was helping me make something out of those old rags that I had been wearing."

"Don't you understand that I am jealous of any man that looks at you? Let alone some nigger boy cutting his eyes at you, I just can't take it."

"I see that, honey. But I am telling you that there is nothing going on with me and that boy down at the nigger bar. He just showed me a trick to an old song that will keep us here for a couple more days, that's all."

"That's all?"

"That's all, my love."

Carolyn kisses her husband and hugs him closely. While hugging him she thinks about the boy at the piano and can't help but wonder about him and his many talents as a musician and as a man. Her husband also knows her a little more than she thinks and knows for a fact that this will end up like the last time. Of course, he could have been wrong about the last man he accused of being with his wife, but this time he is sure that something will eventually happen that will make him do something. He knows that he should be saying something to her, but in his eyes, it's not her that is the problem, it's all the men that find her attractive.

The morning comes, and Walter and Elijah wake up and get the day started. Elijah cleans up the beds as Walter gets ready and walks outside. Walter turns to Elijah, who seconds later walks out of the shack and says, "So what time you think you are going to take me over to see that Kimberly woman?"

Elijah looks at Walter with a frown while Walter stands there with a joking grin. "Now I done told you about minding yourself about Kimberly. She is a well-respected woman around here, and I don't want you around her if you're going to act like a dog in heat!"

"I'm just messing with you, Elijah. I will be on my best behavior."

"Good. Cause I'd hate for you to embarrass yourself in front of her. You'll never get another chance with her again if you do. Now come on!"

Elijah walks with Walter to the store that is run by Ms. Kimberly. They get to the door of the store and Elijah says to Walter, "Now remember what I said about minding yourself around Ms. Kimberly. She is well respected and you only..."

"I know, I know, you only get one chance. Look, preacher man I have seen some of the most beautiful ladies that this land has to offer. I'm sure I will be able to mind myself."

"Okay."

Elijah walks into the store with Walter following behind. The store is modest with the basic of needs for people to purchase. Grain, rope, preserves... all the things that people in this town will need in order to live. Walter is amazed because this is the first town that he has ever been in that had a black person running it. He walks around the store looking at all of the things that she is selling and the things that he will need. He can hear Elijah talking behind him, but has not focused all the way in on the person that he is talking to. Elijah calls out to him, and he turns around to see a woman that is far more than just the word beautiful. Her eyes pulled Walter in right when he looks at her. He thinks he has himself under control as Elijah introduces him.

"Kimberly, this is Walter. He just bought the land next to me and asked if I would bring him here to introduce."

Walter stares at Kimberly because she is so attractive, she is about 5'5 with a caramel complexion. Her eyes are a light brown and very apparent. She opens her hello with a smile that Walter has never seen before and it makes him excited and nervous at the same time.

"Hello Ma'am, my name is…"

He goes to talk to her but knocks over a small stand, full of candy. It hits the ground and rolls all over the store floor making noise as it comes to a stop. There is a moment of silence where Elijah just shakes his head in a silent laugh as Walter finishes his sentence while picking up all of the fallen candies. "My name is Walter,ma'am. I'm sorry about your store."

"That's okay. I hear that you have some money, so I will just put you in the books for a jar of candy."

Walter is still on the ground trying to pick up the rest of the candy frantically as Kimberly says, "You can stop picking up the candy now. Unless you're going to take it all home?"

"I figure since I dropped it and you are making me pay for it, the least I could do is clean your store."

"Well, that is very kind of you, but I was just messing with you. You don't have to buy all of that candy, it's hard candy so I can wash it off and sell it." "No ma'am. I dropped all of this, it's the least I could do."
"Okay, well you just bought yourself a jar of candy. Is there anything else that you would like to purchase since you are here?"

"Yes, Ma'am. I will be building a house soon, so I will need some things to make that happen. Nails and such. I would also like to order some building equipment like hammers and saws also. And a little jerky, some preserves and..." Walter points to a fabric that is sitting on a shelf.

"That there for clothes making."

"That's an expensive fabric. You must really like the woman you are buying it for."

"Well, I kind of do."

Walter hands Kimberly money to cover all of his expenses for the day including the things he has ordered. Kimberly is in shock because most people just owe her for their purchases. This is the first time someone has come in and given her cash on the spot.

"Well, I don't have some of the stuff you want, so it will take a couple of weeks to get here."

"That's okay. I trust you."

"Mr. Walter you don't even know me. Why you trust me with your money?"

"A woman with eyes as beautiful as yours has to be trusted." Kimberly smiles as Walter tells her how beautiful she is. Then changes the subject quickly to try not to let on her interests.

"And what about this fabric? I'm sure the Mrs. of the house would not like you trusting me with your money like that. Especially since you are in here buying her expensive cloth for a dress."

"Well, if I was married, I'm sure she would have something to say, but since I'm not, I think it will be okay."

"Well, who are you buying this fabric for?"

"For a woman that I hope to have a chance to get to know and maybe one day she will have a problem with how I spend my money."

Walter hands Kimberly the fabric and says nothing more about it.

"Now, there is one more thing that I would like to buy, but I don't seem to see it here in the store."

Elijah trying to break up the chemistry between the two says, "And what's that?"

"Bullets. I need some bullets for my guns so that I can do a little hunting and such."

Kimberly and Elijah look at each other with a look of confusion. They have never known or seen a negro that owned a gun before.

"Well, Mr. Walter, we don't have bullets here because we can't sell guns."

"And why is that?"

"Well, the white man say that we can't have guns unless we are hunting. But you have to rent that gun from a white person you know. We are not allowed to have guns of our own."

"Well, I guess that is a good thing then," said Walter.

"What is?" asked Elijah.

"The fact that I will save a lot of money from not having to rent guns, and since you can't have guns it shouldn't worry the white man if you ask him for a couple of cases of bullets."

"Well, I guess I can try," said Kimberly.

"And if you do get them I will spend a little more money for them. You have a good day, Ms. Kimberly, thank you for all of the supplies and candy."

Kimberly smiles at Walter and says, "You are welcome, Mr. Walter. If you need anything else, you just let me know."

"I will Ms. Kimberly, I wouldn't want to ask anyone else."

Walter walks out of the store with a smile while Elijah looks on with a sense of concern. When they get outside of the store, Elijah says to Walter, "So you have guns, huh? We will be needing a sheriff soon. We had a murder here not too long ago, and the sheriff says that he doesn't mess in nigger matters. You think you would like to be our sheriff," asked Elijah.

"Can the Sheriff have a gun?"

"No."

"Well, I guess I am the man for the job."

They both get a laugh out of what was just said and walk toward the church.

You know it's a funny thing about this town, for years we have been trying to be our own city within a city, but for some reason, the white man won't let us. They tell us that we aren't born smart enough to run our own community, they tell us that

we can't own our own stores and shops and hotels because all
we will do is mess things up. And that a nigger with money is a
dangerous one because once he gets it, he will look at himself
as if he were white and that wasn't right. For a long time we
have settled for what they have told us, for fear of what they
would do and some of us just flat out believed it. Well, I feel
something happening in this town of Marthasville. Not your
normal stuff either, something that will change the way we think
and live from now until the end of time. I just hope that I live
long enough to see it. The day when the black man can stand
up for himself and be responsible for his own actions.

Walter gives me hope in that regard. Him being one of those
Union officers that walked pass here years ago on a mission
for our freedom, shows me that there is some hope for us as a
people. That we can fight and govern ourselves without the
help of any other race. Hell, everyone else is allowed to have
their own towns and government. I wonder what makes it so
different for the nigger to do the same? Sometimes I sit up and
watch the town late at night, and I have noticed that this town
still is moving when the sun is sleeping, there is a change

coming, I'm not sure what it is but something is coming that is going to change the way we think of ourselves as a whole. We have been told for years about the things that we can't do, now it's time for us to show the world what we can do.

Chapter 5

Mrs. Lesure is riding in a horse-drawn carriage, driven by one of her workers to visit Catherine at her home. Mrs. Lesure has decided that since Catherine always comes to visit her at her home, that this time it would be a little different since her husband is out of town that she go visit. It is just now getting dark on the plantation, and as Mrs. Lesure looks over into the fields. She sees that Catherine's niggers are still working, which is common but the difference is that they seem to be happy. Almost as if they are working for something bigger than their plantation owners. There are children playing amongst the adults in the fields, and there is no overseer as far as she can see. "How is she keeping them in line?" says Mrs. Lesure to herself. They drive all the way to the front door of the house. Mrs. Lesure notices now that some of the help are surprised to see her and start running toward that house as if to warn Catherine about who is coming to visit. Mrs. Lesure looks over at her driver who is a negro male and is suspicious of the fact that he is acting as if nothing is the matter with what they are seeing. He almost is acting as if he is ignoring it. So Mrs. Lesure turns to him and says, "It's such a nice night out, isn't it?"

"Yes ma'am, it is," replied Emmet.

"I wonder how Catherine gets her workers to stay in line without an overseer in sight.

What do you think, Emmet?"

"Ma'am?"

"I said, what do you think about them not having someone watching over them?" "Ma'am there is always someone watching over them, just not an overseer, ma'am."

Emmet looks up into the sky as Mrs. Lesure looks at him for more of an answer. But he doesn't give one, forcing Mrs.

Lesure to look up into the stars as well. They finally reach the front door of Catherine's home where she and her house servant is standing, waiting to receive their unexpected guest. Catherine is calm and ready to greet Mrs. Lesure, however, her servant stands there rubbing her hands together as if she is somewhat nervous. Mrs. Lesure notices that instead of sending the servant off into the house, she holds her hand as if she is someone that is very important to her. Mrs. Lesure seeing this becomes somewhat jealous about it, but before she decides to speak on it, she wants to make sure that she is right.

"I have always loved the sight of this plantation, Catherine, that I thought I would come and visit you instead."

"And we are so glad to have you here, my maid servant here just let me know that you were coming and I have to apologize because we were not expecting such a wonderful guest. I don't have anything prepared for dinner or anything like that, but we will fix that."

"That is quite alright seeing as I didn't tell you I was on my way. I'm sure that you can have her make us something to eat."

The woman looks at Mrs. Lesure as if that is not something she does. However, she looks again at Catherine for a response.

"Florence, could you please go inside the house and make our guest something to eat." "Make sure that it's chicken. I have always loved the fried chicken that you have made for us over the years," said Mrs. Lesure.

The servant looks at Mrs. Lesure as if she is almost insulted by her comment, looks at Catherine again and proceeds to go into the house.

"Did you see that look she just gave me," Mrs. Lesure asked.

"Yes, I did."

"I have never been looked at with such disgust, let alone by a nigger maid."

"Please watch what you say about my maid, she is very important to this home and the reason we are still able to keep our home after my late husband passed."

"Well, I'm sorry for offending her, I didn't know she was that important to you."

Mrs. Lesure and Catherine go into the dining room and wait on the food that is being prepared in the kitchen. Catherine has something to tell Mrs. Lesure but doesn't really know how to address it, so she asks around the question.

"I want to thank you for coming here and visiting for a while. I wish you would have sent word that you were coming. I would have been more prepared for you, but I do want to talk to you in private, and this seems better than anytime we have before, so."

"Look, Catherine, I have told you that we can't be together. I have a husband and the world is just not ready for two well-respected ladies to be in a public relationship."

"I understand your point and agree with you totally, but that is not the reason I want to talk to you."

Catherine's maid comes into the room with the food that she has prepared for Mrs. Lesure. Mrs. Lesure sits and is served the food she requested, but as the maid is about to leave Catherine signals for her to stay. She is an old woman which is something Mrs. Lesure could not tell in the dark outside. She looks as if she has had a very hard life, she has strong worn hands that she rubs when she is nervous. And her face is full of wrinkles as if her tears over the years have made grooves in her expressions. She keeps her head down in a submissive manner, however it seems as if she has a proud aura about herself. Mrs. Lesure looks surprised because she has never seen a servant allowed to be around in an important conversation. Catherine proceeds to talk.

"I know what your husband feels about colored people and their place in the world, but I want to ask you about your feelings on the matter."

"What do you mean? I mean the war is over, so they are free, and they get to work for their keep like anyone else in the country."

"Except they are paid on a fixed rate so that they can never really gain any money to leave let alone to buy some land. And if they try to leave the area for any reason other than what their plantation owner allows, they are subject being put in jail. Do you ever stop to think what life would be like if you and I were treated the same way for what we believe?"

As Catherine is waiting on Mrs. Lesure to respond the maid servant becomes attentive to the answer that Mrs. Lesure is about to give. "You know, I have never really thought of it that way."

"Have you ever wondered how I kept this place running for the past five years after my husband passed away? How I managed not only to keep this place going but also buy more than fifty more acres of land in the last couple of years?"

"I thought that the bank and the men in the county were trying to help you stay here. My husband said he even came to try to help you once, but you refused."

"No, your husband came here to see if he could buy me out before the land went under. He even tried to buy the land for half of what it was worth. Martha here was the one that showed me that I could do it myself, and with the help of her husband and the people here working in the fields we managed to keep this place going."

"But isn't that some type of slavery? You have them here working for free so that you can stay open doesn't seem to be fair to me."

"I know. Which is what I really what I want to talk to you about. What if I told you that most of the people here were not here two years ago? What if I told you that I was helping colored people to the north? Giving them day passes so that they could get to certain places and disappear, or giving them shelter from where they escaped from, until people stop looking for them?"

"Well, I would think that you are doing something that is against the law, and if anyone was to ever find out, you and everyone here would be in a lot of trouble."

"That's also how they would feel if they ever found out about you and I being lovers." The maid servant Martha is now looking Mrs. Lesure straight in the face as Catherine finishes her sentence. She is embarrassed that Catherine would even bring up the affair that they are having in front of the help.

"Well, I don't think that is any of her business."

"Well, no it's not her business, but it does help her feel a little better about what I have just told you. You see we couldn't take the chance of you going back home and telling your husband about what is going on here. So I have told them all, and I am willing to talk myself if that was to ever happen."

"Why? Why would you go to such lengths to help them?"

"Because they are people just like you and I who would have never been here if it wasn't for our people needing someone to do work that they didn't want to, but will take all the credit for it. The same men who will label a woman like you and I crazy or mentally ill because we find each other attractive in a way that they cannot explain. I owe these people my life, Elizabeth."

"Yes Catherine, I understand, but are they worth risking your life for," Mrs. Lesure asked.

"Yes."

There is a small moment that Elizabeth and Catherine look at each other but have nothing to say. Elizabeth now looks at Martha and says to Catherine, "I want to have a private conversation with you. That's if you don't mind."

Catherine looks at Martha and Martha walks out of the room, she quickly returns with tea and then leaves again for goodbye closing the doors of the dining room.

"What made you do all of this for them?"

"I told you they saved me and this plantation. I was weeks away from having to give the property back to the banks. All the men in the county came here to either ask to buy me out or my hand in marriage so that they could have it, but as you know, I don't have a real interest in the men in the town. So, one day as I sat here crying trying to figure out how I could save my land, Martha and her husband came and shared an idea they had. Martha told me that her husband was good with the crops and livestock and knew how to buy and sell by watching my late husband for 10 years at the trading post. As we started to get this place back up and running, Martha came to me with a problem. Her brother was being chased through the state of Florida, because after he watched his owner rape and kill his wife, he decided to run. For the most part, this has just been a channel to the north for them. Giving them a place to hide, and when the time was right, get them just a little further to freedom. Then during the war, some of the colored men would go out at night and take some of the rifles and revolvers from the fallen confederate soldiers that had passed

95

on. They brought them back here to train with them, and now we are doing special missions for families in need."

"What is a special mission?"

"Well, since the ending of slavery it seems that the government has found a new way of keeping colored people at their feet. By making rules that if they do certain things that a white man does every day, they can be jailed for. Or helping one of their relatives in a state where white people aren't ready to accept change, keeping their slaves by force to stay on their farms."

"So what is in it for you?"

"Well, those people in turn, come here and work off what they have asked of us. They stay for one or two years to help the farm stay up and running, and after that, we make passage for them to the north," said Catherine.

There is a small pause in the conversation as Elizabeth is now looking out of the window. She asks Catherine without looking at her. "I have one last question for you."

"Anything."

"Did you really love me or was it all for this moment?"

Catherine gets up out of her chair and walks over to Elizabeth.

"My husband passed away five years ago, I have been in love with you for the last the last 10 and have always loved you. Now more than ever, but I also was shown that if I am concerned about my rights as a woman, to be free in this country without abuse or ridiculed, I had to be concerned about the people who are being punished for their color and beliefs.

These people had every right to leave me to the wolves, and they didn't. They made sure that we are still here growing strong. I only thought it was right to return the favor. Okay?"

Elizabeth shakes her head in agreeance with Catherine. They hug for a moment and then Catherine says, "So would you like to see how it works?"

The Lake

Mrs. Lesure and Catherine walked out of the back of Catherine's home where a small paddle boat was waiting for them. Catherine with the help of one of the men on her farm gets onto the boat and turns to Mrs. Lesure to help her. Mrs. Lesure wasn't too sure of getting on the boat. She remembers what her father once told her about this lake at night as if it were yesterday.

"Baby girl you can go anywhere that you want, but there is one thing that I want you to be mindful of when it gets dark around here, and that is the lake," said Mr. Johnson. "Why daddy?" asked Elizabeth.

"They say that the end of the lake at night, right over there by those two dead trees there is a witch that only comes out to

98

sing after dark. And they say that if you are in a boat on the lake while she is singing that the lake will swallow you whole."

"Father, do you believe in this story?"

"Yes, Lizzy I do. Your grandmother and her mother tell the same story about a little girl who wandered in there one night returning from her aunt's home and overheard the witch singing in the lake. She liked what she heard so much that she took the boat and left on the dock out into the lake and was never seen or heard from again. Now, I don't want you to be another person that gets taken by the lake so stay out of there."

"I will, Pa. I won't go in there ever!"

"You promise me, baby girl?"

"I promise."

Catherine gets Elizabeth's attention by calling her name so that she can get into the boat. She closes her eyes and takes

Catherine's hand and sits in middle row. They row up the lake and say nothing to each other as the man gets closer to the two dead trees at the back of the lake. The closer they get to the trees the more nervous Elizabeth gets remembering what her father told her and what she promised him. They reach the back of the lake, and that older man gets out of the boat, walks over to what looks like a small tree stump and uncovers something that almost looks like a railroad switch to Elizabeth. He pulls that handle and the further he gets to the other side of the lever a small entrance opens behind the trees, just enough for the boat that they are riding in can get through. He gets back into the boat and rows it to the other side of the small river that has been shown to them. He gets back out of the boat and closes the levy, then proceeds to row further into the lake. Elizabeth is surprised because her whole life she thought the lake stopped where the two dead trees stand, but she is being shown this evening that things aren't what they seem to be. As she sits and watches the area from where she has come Catherine notices her and starts to talk to her in a very low voice. "A long time ago when the negro was not allowed to read from the bible and pray they would come back behind the dead trees to strengthen their faith. They would come back here for years before white men even noticed the lake. Then in order to keep them from exploring more, they started a rumor about a witch that would sing at night and a little girl that wondered to far and was never seen again. What they were hearing was them singing in praise of the Lord. Songs that they had made up themselves to lift their spirits to deal with what they had been going through. We are the only two white people that have ever been back here."

Elizabeth notices the sounds of the water being pushed to the side from the paddle. The further they get away from the entrance of the back of the lake the man rowing the boat starts to hum. The farther they get, the louder he becomes, Elizabeth is worried for a moment that someone will hear them until she notices a small light coming from further down the river. The louder he becomes, the more lights start showing until it reveals a small house sitting on the side of the entire lake. They stop and get out of the boat and go into the house where there are negro's that Elizabeth doesn't know and ones that she has seen before. But she is taken aback because the man that seems to be in charge is her driver Emmet. He looks at her and without a word grabs her hand and walks her into the heart of the room. She looks at Emmet and says to him, "I guess I don't have to ask what you are doing here."

"No, but I will tell you anyway because I feel as if I owe you that much. My name is Emmet Patterson, I was a soldier in the Union army in the 6th U.S. Colored Troops and was awarded a medal of honor for bravery and courage at the Battle of Chaffin's Farm in New Market Heights, Va. After the war was over some of us were asked secretly by the U.S. government to stay in the south and help the former slaves move to the north or escape from unwarranted arrests," said Emmet. "Unwarranted," asked Elizabeth.

"Yes, Mrs. Lesure. The negro man is always under the threat of jail since slavery is no more. It is the new way of putting our people back to work on plantations with no pay at all."

"Are you saying that a criminal should be paid for his crimes?"

"No, what I am saying is that if a person is to be jailed that it is looked at the same way as if a white man was jailed. The president stated that the judge is to use his own discretion in sentencing someone found guilty. The problem is that most men and ladies of color that are convicted of crimes will be sentenced to larger charges in order to keep them behind bars, sometimes for good. So for those who have been put away for false charges we send someone to retrieve them."

Elizabeth laughs a little to herself before responding to Emmet.

"You expect me to believe that you send men to places to rescue people that you believe are innocent of crimes and punishment. How do you do that with your bare hands? We both know that there is no store that will sell guns and ammo to a negro!"

"You're right, but what you are failing to remember is that the first jobs we were given in the army was to make guns and bullets. They won't sell them to us, but they taught us how to make them in the first place, saying that we weren't fit for the battlefields. So knowing what we know about guns from making them ourselves, we teach each other in these woods how to shoot."

"How? I have been here for my whole life and have never heard a gun go off in these parts of the town."

"That is because we try to do it during the daytime when people are less concerned about a gun around here, and we take potatoes' and put them over the barrel of the guns. It helps them silence the bang a little better."

Emmet shows Elizabeth how to put the potatoes on the muzzle of the gun and fires into a bag of hay. It makes a small clapping noise that is only heard by the people in the room. Elizabeth is amazed that not only was the noise of the gun silenced, she still can't believe that the man who has been driving her family around for the past five years is the key person in this operation.

"I know that this is a lot to take in all at once, especially when you have been shown different your whole life. Just know that I am doing this because there aren't any other people in the world that will help our cause."

"So you are telling me that the president himself orders for you and some others to stay down here and help the negro."

"No. I am telling you that there are others in high places that feel as if we are people, just like anyone else. The president's reasons for a civil war was to make this country rule under one set of laws. It was never to free the slaves from the south."

"I never thought of it that way."

"Most people never do when it's not them being treated bad. This is a people problem when all the people finally see it that way is when things will change. We have some new volunteers coming in this evening. Would you like to see how we train them?"

"Well, I have seen this much, a little more isn't going to do any harm."

Emmet takes Elizabeth's hand again, and they walk out of the house. Meanwhile, standing on the outskirts of the town, Matthew and Mark are waiting for something or someone to show them the way to something that will change their lives forever. Feeling a little concerned because it is after dark, Mark says to Matthew. "Brother, what are we waiting on?" asked Mark.

"The letter I got said that there would be a woman carrying a chicken that will lead us to the entrance," said Matthew.

"Now what kind of mess is that? Why would a woman be walking around the town at this time of night?"

"I don't know?! I'm just following the orders of what the letter told me."

"Let me see the letter." Says Mark.

"I can't."

"Why?"

"Because it also said that I needed to burn it as soon as I finished reading it."

"So you're telling me that we are standing here waiting on a woman with a chicken, and the only information we had was in a letter that you burned after reading it?"

"Yes."

"I don't think there is any better time to ask you than now. Have you been drinking a little more than you normally do?"

"Would you be quiet, it's bad enough we are out here at this time of night waiting. There is no need to bring any attention to us."

"You're right, but I think we might be a little too late."

Just then a white man comes out of the supply store, he doesn't turn on a light, but he does have a pistol in hand. He walks quietly over to the two boys and says to them, "What in the devil are you two doing out here at this time of night?"

"Sorry, sir but we were waiting on our auntie to get here from Mississippi. She took a late train in and had to walk all the way from the big city to get here. We thought it would be smart to meet her here so she wouldn't have to walk through the woods alone," said Matthew.

"Well, you better get on out of here before someone sees you." The store owner starts to walk away, and the twins begin to feel as if they were sent on a fake mission.

"Well, I guess we should have kept that letter because we must have missed something," said Mark.

"No, I looked on both sides of the letter, and it said to meet here at this spot."

"Well, we are here, and they aren't and if it was real why would they have us meet them in the white part of town? Why wouldn't they meet us on our side of town?"

"I have thought about that, and the only reason I could come up with was that they wanted to see what we were willing to do. Testing us to see if we were really going to be a part of this."

Just then the store owner softly talks to them from across the street. "PSSST!"

The boys look over at him but do not say a word because they don't want to be heard by anyone else.

"Seems your aunt has been waiting on you, now get out of here before someone sees you," said the store owner.

The store owner points to a little old lady standing at the edge of town with a chicken in her hand. She does not say a word, only waits for the twins to meet her where she is standing. The boys walk at a fast pace to meet with the woman and tip their hats to the man who pointed her out. But before they can get all the way to her she turns and starts to walk toward the woods. They keep a calm pace knowing the man who just saw them is still watching, which allows the woman to stay in front of them at a generous distance. The further away they get from the town, they notice that the woman is walking right into the forest that is supposed to be haunted by a witch. Mark and Matthew are familiar with the story, however, Mark is the only one that still believes it. Matthew gets a kick out the fact that this is his brother's greatest fear. The fear of not knowing what is to come or what has already been. The closer they get to the forest, the more nervous Mark becomes. He starts to doubt what they are doing and says to his brother, "You think it's safe for us to be following this lady? I mean she hasn't even said a word to us," says Mark.

"Didn't you say that this is a challenge? That they are testing us to see what we are willing to do in order to be apart of this? Well, it's either going to make a man out of you or scare the hell out of you tonight."

The woman slowly walks to the outskirts of the forest and looks back to make sure the twins are still coming. She looks at them until they get close enough and walks into the forest with a small light that you can only see if you are a certain distance from her. They keep following her in silence until they get to an open area that only has a small candle in the middle. The old lady walks past the very low lit candle, and four men walk out. The boys stop as they see them and one of the men kicks out the light of the candle. All four men at the same time go after the twins and are instantly met with organized assault from them. They seem to pick the group of men apart easily with their background training from their uncle, so much so that Matthew starts to laugh during the battle. They finish up the last man standing and are finally met by the barrel of a revolver that Emmet is holding. They both freeze at the sight of the gun thinking that what is happening is about to be over real fast.

Emmet says to them both, "I see that you guys are very good at protecting yourselves with your hands, but I see we need to work on what to do when you see a gun," said Emmet.

Chapter 6

Walter and Elijah - (September 4, 1897) - "Swearing in."

Even though the war was over and we are supposed to be free, doesn't mean that they want to have to deal with the negro and their problems. So to our surprise, when Kimberly asked Walter about being the new sheriff for our town, when he said yes he actually was serious. So two months after we asked him we were asked to bring him so that he can be interviewed and sworn in by the sheriff in the city. Sheriff Thomas was a very large man, he had a scar on the left side of his face from a robbery he tried to stop when he first started as the law man of the town. Only a hand full of people know what actually happened to him, but they say that it was from the gun of a man who was trying to rob the local bank in town. As the men who robbed the bank tried to get away, he ran into the street to stop them on their horses. They tried to run him down, and as they went passed him he shot two of the three men. The last one turned and fired his gun hitting the sheriff in the face. He has run this town with an iron fist for years now and does not feel at this point in his life that he should have to worry about any problems in the "nigger" community. So, he has decided that the right person for the job is Walter, being as that he has a military background and honestly because he was the only one to apply for the job. The sheriff's office is a small one with rifles chained to the rack on the wall and a couple of wanted posters next to it and a small desk in the middle of the room. There is a window that faces the town where another man sits in silence cutting and eating an apple. Walter sits in the chair in front of the desk as Elijah stands close to the door. Elijah knows already how things can be on this side of town, let alone in this office with a sheriff who is not too happy with having Negroes around.

"Well Walter, the day has come that we have to bring you in as the first sheriff of Marthasville. Seem to me and the senators of this great state, feel that there is a big problem in the Negro part of town. Now I'm not one to meddle in Negro affairs, no sir.

But what I do know is that this problem has to be solved, and that is where you come in boy. Now, I don't want you to think for one minute that we don't know about your time with the Union army during the war. Hell I was against you even setting foot into this office for that reason alone. But Festus here has brought back to my attention that we don't care what goes on in your town, so we don't care who we appoint as sheriff either. Do we now, Festus," asked Sheriff Thomas.

The man sitting in the chair next to the window finally looks up with a smile on his face and says, "That's right, sheriff, nigger problems are nigger problems, is what I always say," said Festus.

"Well, sir I want to thank you for allowing me the chance to do something like this. I understand that you don't want to be bothered with nigger affairs and that is something we know. However, I was wondering since you are allowing me to be sheriff in Marthasville that we may have a gun of some sort so that I can defend myself as sheriff," said Walter."

"Now there you go, boy, with those wild thoughts about the negro man having a gun to use. What would you need a gun for anyway? It's not like you will have those types of problems. What we want you to do is just report back to us if you see anything happening. Come back to town and tell us about it and we will do the arresting and things, okay," said Sheriff Thomas.

"So, what you want me to do is go back to Marthasville and only come back and report to you if I see or hear something you two men would like to know about, is that right, sir?" "That is exactly right, Walter. Hell, I thought this was going to be harder for you to understand."

"That's because he was a nigger army officer. If he don't do anything else he knows to
listen to orders, right boy," said Festus.

Walter slowly turns his head toward Festus, he shows in his facial expressions that he did not like that comment but the only person to see it was Elijah being the only person in the

116

room actually looking Walter in the face. Elijah is now concerned about what Walter will say next, so he steps toward him and puts his hand on his shoulder to calm him. Walter looks up at him and says to the sheriff.

"That's right sir. I have one last question to ask if I may?"

"Go right ahead, boy," Sheriff Thomas told Walter.

"Would it be okay if I had a deputy? Someone that I could have to help me fight the battles in our town seeing is that I don't have a gun to use."

"That is an excellent idea, Walter. But you were the only one to sign up for the job. If we had someone else to swear in with you we would, but there seems to be no one around."

"Well sir, if you don't mind I would like to appoint someone, seeing as that is something that I could do if needed."

"Okay, well they have to be approved by me, and that would be something we would have to do today seeing is that I need you down the negro part of town and not up here in our roads."

"And I understand that sir, so if I may, could I appoint Elijah here as the deputy?"

There is a small pause in the conversation being that this is all new to Elijah who had no plans of having anything to do with this. Walter and Elijah focus in on each other without a word, yet it almost seems as if they are having a conversation about Elijah's decision. Sheriff Thomas and Festus look on for Elijah's response all while knowing he is the pastor of the Negro church. Festus laughs a little to himself knowing that Elijah will say no and that he is afraid of him in a way. Walter also sees what Festus sees and stands directly in between the two so that Festus can not look at Elijah and says, "Elijah now look at me, I don't normally ask people for things, and I know that this is not the time to be asking you for such a thing, seeing your being a minister and all. But I need someone that I know will have my back if I needed them. Someone who already knows the land and the only person that I can think of is you. Now I understand if you say no, but I really need you right now," says Walter.

"I am here only to do God's will, not to be an officer of the law trying to combat sin with violence. I appreciate you asking me and having that much faith in me to want me as your deputy, but I will have to say no to you and hope that you understand."

Walter turns to the sherriff and says to him, "Well, I guess its just me. You were right sheriff, no one else wants to really help with nigger problems."

"I'm glad you understand, Walter. Now let's gone get this over with before supper, huh?"

"Yea, let's get this-thing-over with."

The sheriff walks toward Walter from behind his desk, he looks down at the bible sitting on the desk and does not pick it up. He stands in front of Walter and puts his hand up to say the oath.

Walter asks Sheriff Thomas, "Are we not going to need the bible, sir?"

"We would, but we don't have a bible available."

"There's a bible sitting on your desk, sir."

There is a small pause in the air, and then Festus looks up at Walter and says, "What he means is that we don't have any nigger bibles around."

Walter stands in front of Sheriff Thomas and is sworn in on this day as the sheriff of Marthasville. Elijah is somewhat unhappy with himself for not helping Walter, however he feels what he has done is what God would have wanted him to do. There are some things that should never mix with religion and Elijah knows that this is one of those times. He will help his friend as much as he can although Elijah does not accept the job as Walter repeats the oath to the sheriff. Elijah silently says the same oath to himself saying that he will do whatever he could within God's order to help him. He knows that Walter will not make it without him. Not because of what he knows about the area, but his blessing from God that will get him through. Once they finish the oath, Sheriff Thomas walks behind his desk and goes into a drawer and pulls out an old rusted badge and throws it on the table for Walter to pick up. He looks at it for a moment and then picks it up and proudly pins it onto his chest. Festus laughs at the fact that this negro thinks that he is a lawman and walks out of the sheriff's office shaking his head. Walter turns to the sheriff again and says to him, "Thank you, sir. I will do the job the best I can. Now, is there any way that I could have a rifle or a gun just in case something is to happen?"

"Now, why would a nigger sheriff need a gun? You just report back to me anything that you see, and I will take it from there. Okay, Walter?" "Yes, sir. I understand."

Walter and Elijah walk out of the Sheriff's office and hurry to get off of the sidewalk because there are two white women walking passed. Once the ladies are gone, they look up and see the sheriff in his office watching them closely, as if he will keep an eye on them until they are gone from the town. Walter and Elijah turn their backs to the sheriff so that he can not make out what they are saying as they walk out of town. As they walk into the middle of the road on their way out, Walter says to Elijah, "Thank you for coming out here with me to be a part of this."

"I wish I could have been more help to you, but my duties to God are a little more important. But I want you to know that I will help you as much as I can for as long as I can."

"I know that, Elijah."

"How? I left you by yourself in that office back there."

Walter stops Elijah from walking, looks him in the face and says, "I know it because God wants me to know."

Walter walks away from Elijah headed to their side of Marthasville and Elijah stands there in his tracks realizing that

Walter has been listening to him. He can't do anything but smile and runs after Walter with complete joy on his face.

Chapter 7

Nathan and Carolyn

Nathan walks into Mrs. Debbie's bar early in the afternoon to practice a new song he has been working on. Nathan doesn't have enough money to purchase his own piano so Mrs. Debbie allows him to use her piano as long as he helps clean the bar before opening every day. He walks into the bar pressing down on the piano keys as he passes by it to go into the back room and puts on an apron so that he can clean. He brings out a mop and broom and starts to clean as he whistles the new song to himself, dancing around the room in between the chairs and tables as if the mop was a woman. Right outside the bar Carolyn stands and watches Nathan from the open door, having a good time cleaning and singing to himself. He trips over one of the legs on a chair, which Carolyn finds funny and cannot help but to laugh at. Nathan hears Carolyn laughing and becomes embarrassed at the sight of her. He straightens the chair that he has tripped over back under the table, cleans his hands off on the apron that he is wearing and addresses Carolyn.

"Sorry about that ma'am I thought I was by myself."

"No need to apologize, Nathan. I was in the area and decided to stop by and see how you were," said Mrs. Carolyn.

"I'm doing just fine Mrs. Carolyn. Just cleaning a little here and there before we open up later."

"Do you dance every time you clean? If so I know a couple of places that would love to have you."

"No ma'am I was just singing to myself a tune that I wrote about two days ago. I could play it for you if you would like to hear it. I just have to finish picking up after the bar."

"I would like that, but is there any way that I could get a drink? It's such a hot day."

"Sure what would it be?"

"Whiskey if you have some."

"Sure do! Mrs. Debbie got a fresh order, in-last night."

Nathan goes to the back of the bar where the new shipment of whiskey is. He picks up a brand new bottle, and while trying to impress Carolyn, he takes the cork from the bottle with his teeth, getting whiskey into his mouth. He cringes at the taste of it and tries to hide the fact that he does not drink. Carolyn is amused at his almost child-like qualities. As he pours her a drink, she is impressed by his ability to play the piano and create songs that bring life to the piano he is playing. She also knows that without him she is destined to end up back on the road with her husband and their traveling band if she does not learn a new tune. The people in town still love hearing "Nathan's Chopsticks," but Carolyn knows that it will not last too much longer. They will want to hear something else and if she can not, her time in Marthasville will be over. She watches Nathan as he pours her glass and sits down at the piano, he begins to play the keys to his new song and Carolyn is immediately in-love with the sound he is trying to make. She walks over to the piano and sits like the first time they met and watches Nathan's hand placements so that she can remember the base of the song. She figures later if she can remember the main keys she can add her own to it. He finishes the song for her and then sits back a little from the piano to ask her what she thought of it, but before he can get a word out, she offers him a sip of her whiskey.

"No, thank you, ma'am. I don't drink at all-much."

"I know, but you have to start somewhere."

Carolyn looks Nathan in the eyes sensing that he is attracted to her. He on the other hand, knows that only bad things can come from such a relationship, so he gets up from the piano and sits at the table behind him. She follows and sits next to him and slides the glass in front of him. As he fixes his eyes on the glass, the closer Carolyn gets to him without him noticing, Nathan looks up at her, and she says, "It's like anything you do the first time at it. At first, it's not good at all, maybe even bad, but the more you try it, the more you will start to like the way it tastes."

Carolyn leans in to kiss Nathan by slowly and softly inching close to him while talking. They engage in the kiss, and the kiss goes from a nervous one to a passionate one in a matter of seconds. Nathan wonders as he kisses her is she doing it because she likes him or his music. Carolyn's intent is only to get Nathan closer so that he will share his songs, she has no problem with sleeping with black men, having slept with one before as a young woman. He was a slave on a friends plantation that did whatever the ladies of the house told him to do. So being with Nathan kissing him is easy. All she has to do is make him love her, and for the fortune and fame, she feels that it's an even trade. She stops kissing him as if she is embarrassed by the thought of liking it to show Nathan that she cares. She walks a short distance away from him, turns around and says, "I think we may be getting a little too carried away seeing that it's early afternoon and all."

"Yea, I think we better cool down a little."

"Yea, I think that drink might be getting to me."
Nathan gets up from the piano and walks back over to the bar where he begins to wash small glasses that are behind the counter. Carolyn walks over to the bar and starts to tap her fingers against the bar making a drum beat that matches the music Nathan was playing on the piano earlier. He notices the pattern and smiles, it's the first time someone has acknowledged his work in a musical way. Also, at that moment he remembered what Mrs. Debbie said about being careful about what he does with Carolyn and the fact that nothing good can come from them being involved. Nathan slows down cleaning a glass, looks up at Carolyn and says, "So, Mrs. Carolyn I don't mean to pry, but why is it that you come all the way down here to visit me?"

"What do you mean?"

"Well, anything that you may want is in the big part of the city where you live. And I am just a nigger from a small town that knows how to play a few keys on the piano."

"Stop!"

"Stop what?"

"Stop telling yourself that you are just some nigger that know how to play a couple of keys on the piano. You are more than that. You are a great piano player. You have opened my eyes to a new way of creating music, and for that, I am very grateful."

"Well, thank you, ma'am, I really appreciate your kind words. But let's be honest, where can playing this old piano get me other than a couple of dollars here and there."
"But that doesn't mean you aren't good at it. It's just the way things are here in the south. Just don't ever stop playing, and if it's okay, I would love to be able to come down here during the

afternoon and learn me some things. Maybe, I can pay you a little for lessons."

"Mrs. Carolyn, that would be an honor."

"Well, it's a date! Let's meet here again in a week and you can teach me some more of the piano."

"Okay, then this time next week will be fine. I will be here cleaning like I am now."

"Well, I look forward to seeing you then. Thank you for the lesson this week. Here is a little something for you until then."

Carolyn hands Nathan a 10 dollar bill while softly rubbing his hand. He watches her fingers rub back and forth, and as she lets go, he finally realizes she has passed him the money. His eyes light up knowing that this is more money that he will see in a month. The things he could buy and the places he could go if he just helped this lady once a week! He looks up at her and says, "Thank you, but this is a lot of money."

"Well, you are welcome. And if you keep teaching me the piano once a week I will keep giving you money and whatever else you may want."

She leans over the bar and kisses Nathan one last time and says, "Even me. Goodbye, Nathan, I will see you this time next week. I hope you will have something fun to teach."
Carolyn slowly and seductively walks out of the bar looking back at Nathan and smiling. Nathan has fallen for her in that moment and can not wait until he sees her again. She gets into her horse-drawn carriage and rides off toward the big city. Nathan runs, watches her as she leaves and jumps in excitement as he finishes cleaning the bar before Mrs. Debbie arrives. He is in-love, but what he does not know is that him being in-love may cost him his life.

Just as Nathan starts to daydream about what just happened and what could be, Mrs. Debbie walks into the front door with a look of concern. She walks right up to Nathan and asks, "Was that the white woman that was here a couple of weeks ago?"

"Yes, Ma'am."

"What did I tell you about seeing that lady?"

"I know, I didn't invite her either. She just showed up when I was cleaning the glasses and…"

"I don't care what she did! I told you not to mess with that lady!"

"I didn't!"

"Well then why is she in-here?!"

"I don't know!"
"Then why was she here!"

"I don't know. I was dancing and singing a song to myself, and when I looked up, she was here."

Mrs. Debbie looks at Nathan for the truth. She knows that he is a very trustworthy young man and more importantly she knows that he will not tell a lie. She waits a moment to see if he will show any signs of manipulation. He is being honest, and Mrs. Debbie knows he is and is sorry that she got loud with him, but she knows the importance of what she is trying to get him to understand.

"I just want you to understand the importance of you not messing around with that woman. She is going to get you hurt if you don't listen to me."

"Why do you think she is such a bad person? I mean, times have changed, and slavery has been over for the last 10 years. Why are you so concerned about her being evil or wanting to bring me harm?"

"It's not her that I am worried about. The white woman only follows what the white man is teaching. You saw what they did to that young man last year because they said he raped that white woman. Now we know that she was having an affair with him the whole time, but all it took was a lie, and now he isn't here anymore. Hung and castrated by a group of men who refused to believe that one of their women would want to sleep with a Negro man. Don't be next, Nathan that is all I am asking of you. Don't be next."

"I won't Mrs. Debbie, I mean I'm almost 19 years old now. I can take care of myself."

Mrs. Debbie realizes that Nathan is right. He isn't the small little child that she would chase out of her bar at certain times of the night so that he would stop playing the piano and go home and go to bed. He is a man now, but she can't help but worry about the things that she has already seen happen.

"You know, I can remember when you were a small child running around here playing that old thing, wishing that you could stay just a little longer to see what the old timers did after they got drunk. But you are right, you aren't a little boy anymore, and I have to let you live your life. But just like I have watched you grow into the man that you are, I have also watched the world and this town in the same way. And the one thing I do know is that this town nor this world is ready to see a white woman being involved in any way with a nigger."

Nathan does not want to believe what Mrs. Debbie is saying. Times and people have changed because the law has changed is what Nathan thinks of the situation. Maybe Mrs. Debbie is right about being with a white woman, but Nathan's heart will not let him believe it. However, Mrs. Debbie knows the naked truth of race mixing and this town. The rules have always been the same since she can remember, a white man may have a nigger mistress but never the other way around. And the only way a mixed baby is excepted is when the father is a white man. Anything outside of that can and will be looked down on or even punished by death.

Nathan goes back to cleaning the bar as Mrs. Debbie sits in her chair and starts to worry. She shakes her head in fear of Nathan being caught in something that he doesn't know soon will explode in his face. He wonders how he could get in any trouble by helping someone learn the piano? And as long as she comes down their side of Marthasville who would ever know? He knows in his heart that he will continue to see Carolyn despite what Mrs. Debbie is saying, and Mrs. Debbie is sick to her stomach because she knows that same thing.

Chapter 8

Mark and Matthew

For the past three weeks, Mark and Matthew have been practicing their skills in using firearms, but they have been limited to the basic revolver shooting at cans on a fence in the middle of the day. It is not uncommon to hear gunfire in the woods, and in the remote location that Emmet has taken them to so there is no one around for them to be seen. Or at least that is what they thought. Mark and Matthew are picking off cans one-by-one, as Emmet looks on. He is pleased with the progress that the two are making and feels as if he has made the right choice by picking them, and that they are ready for the next step. Matthew fires the last shot hitting the final can. The can jumps off of the gate, spins in the air and lands exactly in the same spot that it was in. Emmet and Mark both look at Matthew in amazement after they finish watching this and Mark says to them, "I did a little extra practicing when you guys were sleeping the other day," says Mark.

"A little! Seems to me you been sleeping with the thing the way you are shooting," says Matthew.

"Yes, either way, I think you two are both ready for the last step of your training."

Emmet

"Last step? All we have done is fought and learned how to shoot guns in the last month. How is that going to help us in helping? We have been fighting all of our lives, and the only thing that has gotten us is in trouble," said Mark."

"You two are very talented with the hand-to-hand combat, which is the most important. In this day and age a nigger with a gun is against the law and if that was the only way you could defend yourself you would be in trouble," said Emmet. "What do you mean by that?" asked Matthew.

"Matthew, the gun was invented by the coward, so that he could protect himself with something more powerful than the fist. It was invented as a tool to inflict bodily harm to someone or something that man would normally not be able to tangle with. Being able to use a gun doesn't make you bigger than the next man. It shows that you do not appreciate and condition what God has already given you to protect yourself," said Emmet.

"And what is that?" asked Matthew.

"Your hands and your mind," said Emmet.

Just as Emmet finishes his sentence, a white male rides up with a gun drawn on the three men. The guns that they have are in their hands, but their backs are toward the man so any movement would cost them their lives.

The man screams to them sitting on his horse, "Alright you niggers put those guns down and slowly turn around! Any

141

sudden movement at all and your nigger brains will be all over this field, do you understand me?!"

Emmet says softly to Mark and Matthew, "I think we better do what he says, men."

They all drop their guns and slowly turn toward the man on the horse with their hands in the sky. Matthew and Mark look at Emmet for the signal to attack the man but he never looks at them, and they both know they are a little too far from the man to get to him before he can shoot. Mark shakes his head in defeat thinking that it's about to be over.

"Now, kick those guns over here so that you don't try anything funny and we are going to walk to town. I'm sure the sheriff will like to know that he has niggers in the forest practicing with guns. I'm sure the good people of Marthasville would love to hear that. Glad I was traveling through before things got out of hand. Now you, what is your name boy?" The man on the horse is talking to Emmet as the twins watch in disbelief. He

142

responds to the man as if he is an uneducated man that is afraid for his life. "Me, sir?"

"Yes you, nigger. What is your name?"

"My name is Emmet, sir. We was just out here foolin' around with these guns here. We don't mean no harm to no one."

"Well, you should have thought of that when you were doing something that no white man would let you do."
"Well, we are sorry sir. And if you just let us go we will go home and never do it again."

"No, I think the good people need to know. Now, get over here and pick up those guns and hand them to me slowly."

Emmet slowly walks over to the man on the horse and picks up the guns. He is trembling in fear as he bends down to get them with the man's gun pointed to his back. The twins stand in awe as they watch Emmet turn into almost a helpless man, as he hands the guns to the man he drops one of them and has to pick it up. "Clumsy, nigger."

Just as he finishes insulting Emmet, Emmet grabs him by the foot and pulls him off of the horse that he is riding. As the two men hit the ground and tussle for the gun, the twins stand in shock. Emmet gets the best of the man and calmly takes the gun and shoots the man right between the eyes. The twins have never seen a negro man shake the hand of a white man, let alone shoot one in the middle of the forest. Matthew goes into a small panic as Emmet reaches down and investigates the body of the dead man, going through his pockets and coat. He finds his wallet and looks through it for identification and money. He does not take the money out of the man's wallet and puts it back into his pocket but keeps the identity card.

"What are we going to do now? I mean don't get me wrong I have always wanted to kill a white person, but I never would actually do it! I mean what are we going to do about this?!"

"We are going to take him a little further into the woods, dig a deep ditch and put him in it."

"What?! And then what are we going to do?"

"We are going to say a prayer. Now you two help me get this man into the woods."

And that is what they did. They helped Emmet move the unknown man to a small remote spot in the middle of the forest where they took two hours to dig a deep ditch with the shovel that was on the saddle off the man's horse. When they were all done burying the man, Emmet says a prayer over the buried man and walks away pulling the horse the man was riding on. The twins stay a little while longer looking at the grave site and say their own prayers for the man and for their future in this journey that they are taking. After they finish they catch up to Emmet quietly and continue on walking toward the lake. They take a couple of steps before Emmet starts to talk to them about what just happened.

"The beginning of slavery started in the early 1500's by men who just did not want to do the jobs themselves. Living in a new land and trying to make a way, it was hard developing acres of cotton with just the family that you have. So they took our ancestors and made them work, which wouldn't have been a bad thing if they were willing to pay them. But they didn't. What they did was make your ancestors work for them for free and killed them if they didn't do what they were told. They fell in love with the way our mothers and aunts looked and took care of themselves. So instead of taking the time out to court them and make them feel loved like any white woman they would encounter, they beat them and took sex from them and made them feel like it was their fault for them as white men to do what they did. And you know what? Those women had babies that those same white men denied and sold back into slavery just so they could save face in front of their friends. And now, we meet a man that comes into our forest and threatens our existence with something you know they don't want us to be doing. Now, what would have happened if I just did what that man had said if we all just walked ourselves into town and told them what we were doing out here? What would have

146

happened to us? What would have happened to what we are trying to do for our people? They would have buried us and our movement just like we did that white man back there. So I don't feel bad for having to do what I had to do back there because it's apart of a bigger picture."

"Yea, and what picture is that?" asked Matthew.

Emmet stops walking and goes into his own pockets. He pulls out his bill fold and shows the twins a picture of two little girls in front of a small house.

"These are my children, and I want them to be able to grow up in this country with the same chances that the next child, white or Indian has. Not to be judged by the color of the skin they are in but by the choices they make to be better people. And if I had to kill a man for that dream, then killing that white man was the least of the things that I would do in order to see it happen. Because that wasn't the first time and it sure won't be the last. Now, let's go. We have to get back to the lake house."

"For what? We have seen everything there. It's just a one-room house with a bunch of old torn up maps in it," said Mark.

"Exactly what we want people to think if they ever were brave enough to go back there.
Now let's go."

They walk back into the woods where the old shack is located and there is nothing different than before. Same room with a table in the middle and the room is full of old torn maps. Emmitt pulls the horse inside the shack and ties it to the table leg. Matthew investigates further and notices that they are maps of not just the current parts of America but other countries as well, including a map of Africa that is placed on the wall. Matthew looks at the map closely and notices that there is a certain spot marked, which looks like Egypt. Matthew knows this because he has seen this map once before in his childhood. He cannot remember how, so he disregards the thought, but he feels that something about that map is close to him and his family.

Emmet lights a candle and puts it into the middle of the table in the room, walks over to each leg of the table and opens a latch releasing the table from the ground. They stand with each other for a moment and right before Emmet starts to talk Mark says,"Yes sir, still the same rooms as before. So what is the big surprise, Emmet? This is the same room you showed us with the white lady."

"Yes I did show you all this room once before, but I did not show you what the room holds. Have you ever heard the story about the witch that is supposed to haunt this lake?"

"I mean who hasn't heard that story? I have stayed clear of this place my whole life because of that story," said Mark.

"Well, if you have heard the story you also know that everytime the tide rises it is believed that the witch has swallowed up another person like it has done for so many years. And because the people of the big city are so afraid of the lake that they never took the time out to really see why the water rises at certain parts of the night."

149

"So what are you saying? There something under this beat up old swamp house?" asked Matthew.

"That is exactly what I am telling you, Matthew. In a few seconds, I will be showing you something that most people will never see in their lifetime. It will be generations before someone comes back-here and finds this and hopefully by then we will be free from the oppression we face every day."

Emmet goes to the last leg of the table and releases it causing the area around the table to spin counterclockwise slowly. It starts to gain momentum as they stand there and notice that the floor of the room is sinking into the water. Mark is taken by surprise and holds on to the table as Matthew stands in awe watching it unfold in front of him. Emmet sees Matthew's interest in the process of what is happening and smiles. He begins to explain what is exactly going on.

"There have been many inventions over time that have been thought of and designed by black men and women for centuries. One of the first recorded inventions that the black man has blessed the world with was not the pyramids and how to design structures and building from rock. It was the concept of irrigation and plumbing, the education of how to run water in a direction that it did not move in naturally. This tunnel is made up of a metal enclosing that looks somewhat like the outer workings of a screw. Below us are 12 people pulling a chain that is attached to a pulley that is lowering us down into the lake. The water is pushed out of the tunnel and into the lake which makes the water rise at the shore, this is the witch that everyone thinks is back here."

The water rushes from the bottom of this tunnel, and the tide rises as Emmet said it would. The further down they get Emmet begins to fill in the blanks as to how this all came about.

"Do you remember John Smith?"

"I think I remember that name. He was known for being able to swim really well. My dad used to talk about him all the time and said that he could hold his breath for over 15 minutes underwater. But he died a couple of years ago from drowning in the river I think, right?"

"Yes and no. John was a great swimmer that is true, but John was also a part of this whole thing being the key to us designing this structure. He died diving for the last time into the lake in order to secure the building that is now waterproof."

"But they found his body in the river about two miles away from here, not in the lake," said Mark.

"We know," replied Emmet.

The platform continues to spin going further down into the tunnel and finally rests at what seems to be the bottom. There are three sounds of latches being opened, and a small door is opened at the bottom for the three men to exit the tunnel. They step out into a gigantic room full of things that Matthew and Mark have never seen before.

Some are familiar but have a different function, there is something that looks like a cotton gin, but it is pressing out another type of material. There are men and women working on different types of guns, mostly small for concealment, but can fire as if they were a .22 caliber rifle being the most powerful gun at the time. Matthew and Mark are in disbelief of what they are seeing and at the same time interested in all of it. They continue to walk, and Emmet stops in front of a man with a white overcoat on. He is a short man with glasses and a small limp. He talks with the best of education and asks Emmet about the two boys, "Are these the two men that you have been telling us about for the past couple of years," asked George.

"Yes they are," said Emmet.

George walks over to the boys to meet them as Emmet takes the horse over to a stable with ten horses in it.

"Well, it is a pleasure and an honor to finally meet you two gentlemen. My name is George, I am an inventor from Virginia and I look forward to working with you in the future."

"Working with us how," asked Mark.

"Well, I come up with new inventions and gadgets to help the cause. Like this coat here. I have just finished it, and in theory, it will stop a bullet at the highest caliber the world has seen."

He shows Mark and Matthew the coat, and they look at each other and somewhat laugh.

"You are telling me that this coat can stop a bullet from killing a man?" asked Matthew. "In theory yes, the ancient Chinese developed a coat of silk that would stop the penetration of a sword, this was known as the first lightweight vest that would protect a man from a sharp object. Giving him a second chance if he was to make a mistake in fighting. I have furthered their findings and added this to the formula, and I think that it will stop a bullet from killing a man if he is hit in the chest," said George.

George goes over to the machine that looks like a cotton gin and pulls a small piece of material from it and hands it to the twins.

"This is Hevea brasiliensis. It is found in South Africa and has been used for years. But I like to call it rubber."

"Rubber?" Matthew and Mark both asked.

"Yes, rubber. It has a million and one properties, in which, it can be used for the soles of your shoes. It's actually more comfortable than the wooden soles you see in today's shoe design. And it also, with the combined sciences of the Chinese, is the base of that material I have formed to stop a bullet in this coat. Would you like to see if it works?"

"Yes I would," said Mark.

"Good then you are my first-ever volunteer for this experiment," said George.

"Wait, what does volunteer mean?" asked Mark.

"That means you offered to help," said Matthew.

"Okay, that's good. I thought it meant that I was going to have to put that coat on and let him shoot me," said Mark.

"That is exactly what that means," said Matthew.

Mark looks down and realizes that George has already put the coat on him halfway and begins to panic.

"Wait, how do I know that this is going to work?"

"We don't," replied George.

"So what will happen if this doesn't work?"

"Then you will die in the name of science."

George by this time has the coat all the way on Mark and is standing in front of him with a small revolver cocking the hammer back so that he can discharge a round. As he squeezes the trigger, Mark yells out.

"Wait!" called Mark.

George fires the weapon directly into the chest of Mark and Mark goes flying across the room. Everyone in the room stops as Matthew runs to his brother's side fearing the worst. Mark is okay, but has the wind knocked out of him momentarily and lays there saying a small prayer to himself.

"God, I just want you to know that I love you, I really do."

"Are you okay," Matthew asked.

"Yea, I'm going to kill George with my bare hands when I can finally get up from this floor, but I am fine."

"Emmet, did you know that this coat would work?"

"No."

"Then why did you let him shoot at my brother?!"

"Because I believe in George and his inventions. He just doesn't believe in them all the time."

Emmet walks away from the twins and goes into another room while George checks on Mark by checking his vital signs and the coat itself. Matthew gets up from the floor with his brother and walks behind Emmet and says to him, "Say, where did you find this crazy inventor anyway?" asked Matthew.

"George was the first person to find a cure for smallpox. He cured his entire town with his formula, but when the whites came to get the medicine, they didn't feel that they should have to pay a nigger for it. So they took his wife and beat her until she died, and when it was time to do the same to George he ran and got caught in a bear trap in the woods. Well, they caught up with him and beat him up, also leaving him in the beartrap to die; and that is when I found him and helped him escape."

"Why did you have to help him? At least they left him alive."

"Yes, they left him alive, but only to come back and have more fun later, when they were liquored up and ready to take all of the deaths that smallpox had caused, out on George over there."

"It's hard to believe sometimes that people are that way. I mean I have heard stories all my life about white people doing some of the meanest and strangest things to Negro men, just because they were Negro. It's hard for me to see why they would want to harm us that way."

"You know I have thought long and hard about that, and the only thing I could come up with is something that George said to me once. And that is spiders."

"Spiders," said Matthew.

"Yes, Matthew, spiders. See, I hate them, I can't even be in the same room with them without being sick to my stomach. So anytime I see one I make it my business to kill it because I don't know enough about them. Well one-day after George had gotten here, a spider-was-crawling across the room. It was a big one, so I didn't think twice about killing it with my shoe. That was until George stopped me and told me about all of the good things that spiders do for us on a day-to-day. Did you know that if it wasn't for spiders that flies and different bugs all over the world would eventually take over the planet, if it wasn't for the spiders trapping them in their webs and eating them?"

"No, but what does that have to do with anything?"

"Well, it was at that moment that I learned something about the spider. And I realized that the only reason I have ever done harm to them is because I never knew anything about them. And that they are God's creation just like the rest of us. Even if there are some that are deadlier and meaner than others. The white man has always treated us the way they have because they have never known any of us as people. We have been their servants and slaves, but never a friend to them. Not because we didn't want to either. It's because they won't let us. One day they will get to know us as people and not property, and when that happens, that will be the day this country really becomes what it's supposed to stand for."

"I never thought about it that way."

"Most people don't. That's why the world is the way it is now. It's time for your last assignment before we send you out into the field.So let's go check on Mark and make sure he is okay."

Matthew and Emmet walk back around the corner to find George listening to Marks vital signs and checking his body to make sure that he is not injured. Emmet walks over to Mark and puts his hand on his shoulder. Without saying a word he looks at Mark and smiles. Then pats' him on the back and walks away. The twins watch him walk away as George says, "He must really like you two because I have seen people lose

161

arms and he doesn't even blink an eye. Well, it looks like you are okay and that the coat works, so everything is okay. Just know that you only get one chance to be shot in the same spot of the coat, anything after that you are at high risk of being killed. I also took the liberty of creating a new pair of boots for you two, and I think that you are going to like them."

He goes around the corner and opens a glass display case with two pair of what seem to look like boots. They have the same style of a normal boot a cowboy would wear, but they have a sole made of the material from the invention George has that creates rubber. He gives them both a pair of these boots, and he waits with an anxious look as if they should know what they are. The twins look at George and wonder what they are holding in their hands. It looks like a boot, but the bottom of the boot looks strange to the both of them. For a moment the twins and George look at each other as if they are waiting on the answer to a question. Finally, Mark asks George, "So George should I ask what these are or are you just going to shoot me?"

"Ha, no you two, these are my latest invention. They are a boot like the cowboys would wear, but instead of having a sole made of leather its made of the stuff I was telling you about earlier... rubber. I call it the RUBBOOT."

"Rubboot?"

"Yes, Rubboot. It's designed to help you grip the ground better if you ever have to run or climb anything. And they are better for your feet, seeing that you two will be walking long distances."

"But they are ugly."

"Science is for solving problems, but that doesn't mean it looks good."

They both put on their pair of boots and walk around in them, trying to get a feel for the way they are made. George waits in excitement to hear what they think of the new invention. The twins are at a lost for words and don't really know what to say to George so that they do not hurt his feelings. They can tell by the look on his face that he is very proud of this invention, but know that George's confidence depends on the approval of his inventions. So Matthew thinks of something that encourages George. Then George asks, "So what do you guys think of my invention?"

"You know what, George? It's the first time that I have ever seen anything like it. And that means that it has to be special," said Matthew.

"Thank you! Emmet is waiting for you around the corner to go back to ground level. I look forward to seeing you again."

They both shake George's hand before walking over to see Emmet. They both walk a little funny over to the area Emmet was in, because they are still wearing the boots George had given them. As they enter the area, Emmet turns to them and begins to talk.

"You two have finally completed the first stages of becoming part of a secret organization that has been going on for the last 200 years. There have been some that have been successful and some that have been killed during missions over the years. But the ones that have made it, all say the same three things that are important in your journey and they are as follows: one, always be aware of your surroundings even in your sleep. Never lay your head or relax your body without making sure that there is no one or no way a person can sneak up on you without you knowing, two, stay away from the main roads until you have to use them. The people that will be looking for you or interested in your travels will not stray too far from the roads that have already been made. Stay close to the heavy forests and away from the flat lands until you have no other options. Even if it means having to walk around instead of straight ahead. If not, it could mean you being seen and possibly losing your life. And finally but most importantly, number three, never and I mean never trust anyone that is not a part of the information that we will give you for your missions. There are people in this world that have good in them, but because of the way this world works with fear and misinformation, even people

165

can be convinced that what you are doing is bad. And always understand that just because they look like you and are the same color doesn't mean that they can be trusted."

"Why would our own people do us any harm? I mean once they find out what we are doing I think they would be supportive and help us as much as possible," said Mark.

"Mark, as much as I love my people in this very town, they all watched your uncle hang from a rope knowing that he did nothing wrong," said Emmet.

"My uncle was hung because he tried to rob a bank," said Matthew.

"No, your uncle was hung for trying to help a friend of his retrieve some money that was stolen from his friend from the very bank that supports this town," said Emmet.

"What," asked Mark.

"The First Bank of Marthasville has over one hundred thousand dollars in it from the businesses and neighboring farms within a 15 square mile radius. However, it accounts for more than one hundred and seventy five thousand dollars in the last year. Do you know why?"

"No."

"Because the seventy five thousand does not belong to the white people of Marthasville nor the bank. It comes from the negro side of town. When they were declared free, the ones who had saved up enough money to try to buy their freedom back were told that their best way to get rich is to save it in a bank so that it would collect something called interest. So, they took their money and did just that and received certificates saying that they had a certain amount of money in the bank that they could check on and withdraw anytime that they would like."

"So what is the problem?"

"The problem was that when those people went back to the bank to withdraw some or just to check on it to make themselves feel important, they were told that they had no money in the bank. And that the certificates they were given were not of any value. Even though less than a week prior they sat in those very seats they were in. So your uncle and a group of men decided that the only way they would get the money back is to take it. And they did it to, without anyone seeing them or getting hurt in the process."

"So how did they get caught?" asked Matthew.

"Well, one of the men that had his money in the bank told the sheriff after he received his money back from the mission. He told them the names of all the people involved because he feared that the sheriff would come and get him if he found out he got his money back. See, fear is why you can only trust a certain kind of person. Color has nothing to do with it, just the courage of a person to be different than the rest. Now, take off those boots and let's go back up the mainland, it's almost morning, and we should make our way up before the sun has risen."

All three men got back into the tunnel that they came down-in, and the door is firmly shut behind them. Five doors open below the floor that they are standing on and water rushes into the tunnel pushing them back up to the small shack that they were originally in. As the water fills the tunnel, the shore line starts to sink, and they are finally back into the room. Emmet hooks the latches back in place on the legs of the table and turns to the boys and says, "Your training for these missions is complete. There is only one thing that you two have to do before we start our journey."

"And that is?" asked Mark.

"Either tell your father a lie or the truth about what you are doing. A lie will get you so far, but the truth will secure your safety as long as you are involved. Think about it and get back here in a week around the same time."

Emmet walks away toward Catherine's home, and the twins go the opposite direction toward the Johnson plantation. As they get further away from Emmet, Mark says to Matthew, "So I was thinking about the lie we could tell Poppa. And I have come up with two, either we can say we are going on a fishing trip or that we are going to visit Aunt Clair up in Virginia."

"No," said Matthew.

"Yea, you are right, just not believable enough for Poppa to not ask about it. Maybe we could say we are joining up with the railroad."

"We are not going to tell him a lie at all, we are going to tell him the truth."

"Why do you always want to do things the hard way? Now you know Poppa is going to lose his mind when we tell him what we are doing. Are you sure that is the right thing for us to do?"

"Yes."

"Okay, well you tell him because I don't feel like getting my ass whooped. I will be 19 in a couple of months and getting my hide tanned isn't something I voluntarily do."

The boys walk as the sun starts to come up for the day. Both ready for whatever is about to come their way, but have no idea the dangers of them. Emmet walks away with an unsure feeling about the twins and what they are here to do in the future. By revealing what he knew about their uncle's death shows that he has more information than he is letting on. And it's just a matter of time before the twins start to ask questions.

Chapter 9

Mr. and Mrs. Lesure - Mr. Lesure returns

The morning starts out a lot like any other morning in Marthasville with the help rising early so that they can get the day started. Some of them are tending to the livestock on the farm, as others begin their day harvesting the fields so that they can get the best chance in the day to meet the required amount of cropping done before the day is finished. There are children playing in the fields as well, running around without a care in the world, not really knowing what type of world they are living in. One of Mrs. Lesure's servants is sweeping the front porch when she looks up and notices a horse-driven carriage coming toward the house in the distance. Riding in the carriage is a tall man that seems like he can not wait to get off of the carriage and relax. It is Mr. Lesure coming home from his political trip to visit with some of the most important men in politics of the time. The maid starts to smile a little as he gets closer and runs into the house to tell Mrs. Lesure that her husband is home.

"Mrs. Lesure! Mrs. Lesure! Your husband has made it home from his trip. He is almost here and looks as if he is tired," said the servant."

"Well, we need to be making him some breakfast and be giving him a nice bath this morning. I'm sure that he must be tired from all that riding he must have done in the last couple of days. Let's hurry and get things together. Tell Margaret to make some breakfast right away," replied Mrs. Lesure.

Mrs. Lesure's servant goes one way as she goes the other taking advantage of the last couple of minutes they have before Mr. Lesure makes it to the house. As Mrs. Lesure sits at a mirror making herself up before Mr. Lesure gets home, she is thinking about all of the conversations and things that she has seen over the last couple of weeks since her husband has been away. It has been a very eye-opening experience for her seeing the world she once knew as being just a little different then most people see it. She brushes her hair and thinks about all the conversations that her and Catherine had since her husband has been gone. She thinks about the secrets that she has learned about the people that have been working for her husband for years and feels as his wife that she should tell him. But in the same thought, she realizes that she has a secret as well that she does not want the world to know about. She worries that because some of the help around the house knows her secret, that they will eventually tell her husband or use it against her to get things that they want. In the middle of her thoughts someone knocks on the door and says, "Mrs. Lesure, your husband has arrived."

She feels a sense of excitement after the maid tells her that her husband has made it home from his journey. And hopes that the secrets she has learned are just as important as the secrets she has told Emmet and Catherine's workers. She gets up from her seat in front of the mirror and hurries to the front of the house to meet her husband as he arrives.

"The love of my life has finally returned to our home! What do I owe this honor seeing is that if I had to wait one more day I was going to call the military in to find you?"

"A hot bath and a big meal will do wonders for me seeing that I have been in-travel for the last four days. But for now, I will settle for a kiss from the most attractive woman I have seen in all my life."

The couple embrace each other for a short moment and almost let go of each other until Mrs. Lesure pulls her husband close once again. He is delighted by the show of affection, seeing how he knows his wife has been distant for some time. He looks at her deeply into her eyes and says to her, "I can not tell you how long I have been waiting for that feeling. Well, I guess I can tell you seeing that it has been exactly a month and three days since I have seen you last. Tell me, have you been bored since I have been gone or have you been running around with that Catherine?"

They begin to walk into their home and up the stairs to their bedroom as Mrs. Lesure says to her husband, "Don't be foolish Timothy. The only thing entertaining since you've been gone are the conversations that Catherine and I have shared."

"Is that so?"

"Yes, it is so, my love. But now I have you back, and I want to know anything and everything about your trip."

"Can I tell you over a hot meal, maybe?"

"Fried chicken already cooking downstairs in the kitchen, I hope that you are as hungry as you say you are."

Mr. Lesure smiles with happiness, because this is one of his favorite dishes made in his kitchen by his servers. He claps his hands and kisses his wife on the cheek once again and says, "I can not wait until it is time to eat. I have been dreaming about this day for some time now. But first I would like to take a nice hot bath."

"Already waiting for you my dear."

Mr. Lesure smiles at his wife once again taking his shirt off and beginning to walk into the bath when there is a knock on the door. Mr. Lesure goes over to the door as Mrs. Lesure sits at her mirror and starts to brush her hair. It is Emmet standing there to Mrs. Lesure's surprise as Mr. Lesure greets him from not seeing him for so long. "Well, look at who decided to come see me after all this time away. You know I have always felt safe when I have gone on my trips to the capital ever since you have got here. Before I used to worry about my lovely wife when I would leave, but now I don't. What can I do for you Emmet?"

"Sir, your new blacksmith is here working on the horses we have down at the stable. He is doing a pretty good job if you don't mind me saying too, Mr. Lesure."

"Yes, well I will be the judge of that. You go ahead, and I will catch up in a minute."

"Yes, sir."

Emmet leaves the room, and Mrs. Lesure just stares at the door in the place that Emmet was standing in. Mr. Lesure thinks that she is staring at him and says to her, "You must have missed me."

"Yes, I have, more than you will ever know."

"Well, my love as always, there is always something to do."

Mr. Lesure walks over to his wife sitting at the mirror and rubs her shoulders as he says to her, "So I am going to run over to the stable and check on the new nigger we have working on our horses. It will only take a little while, not even enough time for the water to get cold."

"Is that a promise?"

"Yes, that is a promise, my love."

"Then I shall wait at the dining table for you."

"Then I will make sure that I take less time."

Mr. Lesure leaves the room as his wife looks at her reflection in the mirror for a little longer. She shows a small expression of sadness as she listens to her husband go down the stairs. She fixes her face once again and continues to brush her hair. She glances over at the door to see Emmet once again standing in the doorway. He says to her, "I know that it may be difficult for you right now seeing as what you have learned about some of us here in the last couple of weeks. And seeing as there is now something that some of us know about you, it probably makes things much more difficult hiding these things from your husband. Just know that we have no intention of saying anything to anyone about what you do in your life as a person. We all believe that is a natural right that all of us should have. Don't worry yourself about us here being or acting any different to you and your home then you have seen your entire life. We

180

will continue to be the way we have always been because we all have the same reasons you have to be here."

"Thank you for saying that, Emmet."

"You are welcome."

Mrs. Lesure watches Emmet as he walks out of the room. "Emmet."

"Yes, ma'am?"

"What reasons do we have in common to be here?"

"So maybe that one-day our cases will be heard the proper way."

Emmet turns and leaves the room while Mrs. Lesure thinks about what he has just said. She is still unsure of her safety, seeing the secrets that seem to be floating around her home. She thought of a time when she and Catherine were the only people that knew their secret and how safe she felt. And even though Emmet has just said something that should comfort her, she can only think about the next time her husband leaves for business and what they may request of her. Is it worth keeping her secrets hidden?

Mr. Lesure walks into the stable as Emmet suddenly catches up to him. Mr. Lesure thinks briefly about Emmet leaving the house before him and should be in the stable before he arrived. He doesn't think much about it knowing that Emmet is very much needed and helpful around the house. He looks at Emmet and chuckles to himself knowing that he is a busy man and wonders what he would have done without him on the plantation. He turns to Emmet and puts his hand on his shoulder and says to him, "So Emmet who is this new blacksmith that you are so head-over-heels for?"

"Sir, this here is Charles Freeman. Folks in town call him Charlie."

Mr. Lesure says nothing back to Emmet and proceeds to walk around the stable and look at the work Charles has done since he has been gone. He looks over one of the horses by lifting its leg to view the shoe Charles had recently put on the horse. He puts the leg back on the ground and pats the horse gently on the back before he addresses the two in the barn. He looks at Emmet and smiles, and then turns to Charles and says, "I don't like it."

"I'm sorry, sir," said Charles.

"I don't like the work you have done, so I need you to redo every shoe that you have
done since you have been here."

"Yes, sir I will get on it right away."

"If right away you mean now, then you are doing exactly what I asked of you. Emmet, I am going in the house to have breakfast with my wife. You see to it that he re-shoes every horse in this stable."

183

"Yes, sir."

Mr. Lesure walks out of the stables and Emmet and Charles just look at each other for a moment until they are sure that Mr. Lesure is gone. Once his footsteps had faded toward the house, Emmet says to Charles.

"Are you okay?"

"Yes, I guess. I really worked hard to make sure every shoe was done right. I just don't understand why he didn't like it." "It's because he didn't want to like it, boy. Always remember there will always be someone who will not like what you do just because you are the person you are. It could be color or opinion, but the point is they just won't like it, so there is no sense in worrying about it."

"Yes, sir."

Charles begins to start over on the horses that he has already put shoes on, and Emmet turns to help him as they both smile about the situation. Mr. Lesure goes back into his home and takes a bath so that he can meet with his wife at the table for breakfast. He finishes his bath and is walking into the dining room where his wife and a couple of the house servants are waiting for him. He sits down at the table, and the servants begin to bring him food as his wife begins to start a conversation. "So my love, tell me all about your trip to the city."

"I don't want to talk about that. Just a bunch of old men talking about what this country should be."

"Well, were there any interesting conversations that you would like to share with me?" Mr. Lesure bites into his favorite dish and closes his eyes as he chews it. He takes a deep breath and smiles before he starts to talk.

"You know there was one conversation we were having that was quite interesting."

"What was that?"

"Well, one of the men in the meeting proclaims that niggers can work and fend for themselves. I say niggers are born to serve and do what we want them to." Mrs. Lesure looks around the room because she knows that some of the people in the room are a part of the organization Emmet belongs to. She looks at the servants one-by-one, but none of them make any expressions or movements as if they are bothered by her husband's statement. She pushes her hair to the side in a nervous gesture as Mr. Lesure continues to talk.

"..And here is why I think that I am right. Since the day they arrived in our great land, they have done exactly what we have wanted them to do, unlike every other group of people that have come here."

"Well, what do you mean?"

"Think about it, ever since the beginning of America all races have fought for their freedom, except the nigger. The English, the Irish, the Mexicans, hell we had to trick the Indians into trusting us, or we would have become *their* slaves. Thank God for foreign disease or Christopher Columbus would have come all this way for nothing!"

Mr. Lesure laughs at himself as his wife gets more and more uncomfortable knowing where this conversation is going. She knows that her husband has little to no respect for the Negro race, and the more that he talks, the more uncensored he will become.

"I mean I have to admit, I have heard that when they first started to bring them over here, they were very proud people. Most of them died coming over here because they kept trying to fight for their freedom, but just like our clever ancestors have done for us so many times they figured out a way to break the spirit of our aggressor."

"How so?"

"Well, the white man figured out that the only way to the male nigger was by getting to the female nigger."

Mrs. Lesure looks at her husband with a puzzled look as she waits for him to finish his sentence. Mr. Lesure looks back at his wife with a smile seeing that she is listening to every word he is saying.

"See, my grandfather told me once about his father and what they did to break the nigger back then. There was a time where they would revolt and fight back all the time when they first got here. Hell, for a little while they thought that they couldn't be controlled and almost gave up on the slavery thing until they started to mess with the nigger woman. See, when a nigger boy got out of line what they would do is tie his legs and arms to different mules and sent the mules into opposite directions pulling the nigger apart. Well, doing this in front of the men only made them fight harder, but when you did it in front of the nigger woman, they would run home and tell their babies that if they fought back that is what would happen to them, making them scared of us before they are big enough to fight back.

188

See, physically they are stronger and faster than we are, but mentally they are like children. Easy to convince and control. Now my love, I am starved! Can we not talk so much politics and just eat?"

"Yes I think I have heard enough, let's eat and just enjoy each others company."

They sit in silence finishing their meal for the afternoon as the rest of the house still is in movement with servants tending to their jobs. Mr. Lesure sits in full appreciation of the meal he is having while his wife sits and picks at her plate. Worried about her view of the negro and who it is changing, as she starts to see things differently.

Chapter 10

Elijah and Walter

Time has passed, and Walter and Elijah have become good friends. Walters house is almost finished, and the church he promised to help Elijah build is finished and a beautiful site to see. It's a small church but is built with love and care, having one big meeting room for worship. But the outside of the church is solid with fine craftsmanship and pride, Elijah and Walter took their time building these buildings that they are very proud of. They also took a little time to build a small jail on Walters property and are inside finishing up the hidden gun rack built into the floor of the jail. Walter is putting the last shotgun into the storage and closing it as Elijah walks back into the room. Walter closes the floors door and puts a small throw over the top of it so that it isn't seen by someone that would just walk in, as Walter signals for Elijah to help him with the desk to sit on top of it. Walter looks at Elijah and says to him as they move the desk, "You know I been meaning to ask you something, Elijah."

"Now if you are trying to be funny again about marrying Ms. Kimberly I told you the answer already. Just because she helped you get some shells for those guns doesn't mean she is interested in you."

"No, Elijah I have a real question I would like to ask you."

"Okay, what is that?"

"Well, I always wonder why us niggers never fought back in slavery. How over 300 years have went by, and we are just getting a small taste of freedom. And not like the other people here in this country who can go and come as they please. We still need permission to travel across the state, let alone the country."

"So what is your question?"

"Well, I guess what I am trying to ask is why do you think we never fought back as a people over all these years?"

"Well, if you ask me, I think that it was a part of our punishment."

"What punishment?"

"Tell me, Walter, when you think about God and his Son what do you think of?"

"Well, I never really thought about it. What do you mean?"
"Well, when God made man, he put them in a paradise that they would be in charge of. God said that they could have it all except for one tree in the area and they disobeyed, right?"

"Right, but what does that have to do with anything?"

"Well, when God saw that they were not listening to him, he told them they would be punished with hard labor and turmoil for years to come. That's why I think our people were slaves for so long. We are paying for the original sin since we are the original man."

Just as Elijah finishes his sentence, the sheriff and his deputy Festus walk into the jail without knocking or saying anything. Festus comes in and starts looking around the room almost in disbelief in what they have built in the town. The sheriff looks at the two men and says to them, "Nice place you two have built here. Almost looks better than our jail in town."

"Well, thank you, sherriff. We just wanted to have something, in case we do-run into any trouble here."

"Well, that's nice to know seeing that you will report anything and everything to us, and anyone that needs to be in jail will be jailed in town with the real law of the land. But all this is pretty to see."

Festus walks out of the jail laughing at the efforts Elijah and Walter have put together to be real law men in their part of town. Sheriff Thomas waits until Festus walks out of the building before he speaks again to the two.

"You know, I have to admit this place looks pretty good. I didn't expect all this. All you two need is a rack for a couple of rifles, and this place would look like a real jail."

Walter and Elijah looked at each other quickly with their eyes before the sheriff turned back around to look at them.

"But in all honesty, I really don't want you to doing any lawing around here. I just want you to keep your eyes and ears open to what is going on in your town and if you hear of anything just let me know. You don't have to try to get anyone in your new jail. Just let me know, and we will come down and take care of the rest."

"We will do that, sir. Anything we hear around here we will surely let you know about it."

"That is exactly what we want you to do. It's the only way this thing will work, and I am glad that I picked you for the job. Since you people have gotten your freedom, ya'll act like you can do whatever you want sometimes."

"Well, we will do just that sheriff and if you need anything from us you just let us know."

"Just do as I tell you, and everything will be fine. I will be coming out here every now and again to check on things."

"That's fine, we will be here whenever you come to visit."

Sheriff Thomas shakes his head in agreement with what Walter has just said, as he walks out of the jail to meet Festus waiting for him by their horses. They ride away, as Walter and Elijah wave goodbye to them. Then Elijah said to Walter, "This town is pretty quiet. We probably won't see them too much."

Chapter 11

Carolyn's solo act

Carolyn has been seeing Nathan for the past two months now and has learned some of Nathan's songs so that she can remain popular in the city. And it has been working, Carolyn is becoming a very well known piano player in Marthasville and also becoming very rich, seeing as she is selling out audiences every night at the saloon she has been working for. She finishes up another set in the saloon and is given a standing ovation as she says to the crowd, "Thank you for all of the applause you are giving us as a band here tonight. I would like to do a small number that I just came up with not too long ago, and I hope that you all enjoy it as much as I enjoy playing it for you."

Carolyn starts to play a song that none of the other band mates including her husband has ever heard. They sit and try to figure out where she is learning all of these new songs from, but her husband knows all too well what she is doing. The audience is in delight of Carolyn's new song and show appreciation by giving her their undivided attention. Some of them even get up and dance to the slow melody with their partners and wives.

"The days we spend

The times we share

All alone at this piano

Wishing you were there

But through it all I sing out loud

Knowing that you are listening

And hope that you are proud."

Carolyn's husband listens closely to the lyrics of the song trying to find any small connection he can to where the song comes from. He knows that Carolyn has been taking care of them since they have gotten to Marthasville and that the song that saved them from having to move on was the song he heard in Mrs. Debbie's a few months back. And he knows that she is not practicing these songs with the rest of the band so that means they can only be coming from somewhere else.

Carolyn finishes the song, and the audience stands and claps for her for almost five minutes. The ladies in the room are crying from being moved by the song as she gets up and bows. After the show, she is standing in the saloon entrance shaking the hands of the people that were there to hear her. Her husband stares at her, somewhat jealous of her success but more worried about the songs that she is playing. The saloon owner is the last to see Carolyn and shakes her hand like any other night, thanking her for what she has done for his saloon. He signals for her to come to his office so that he can pay her for the night and she agrees. Her husband waits with the rest of the band while she conducts her business. The saloon owner counts out the money she is owed and slides it across his office desk and says to her, "You know you have made this saloon more money in the last two months than it ever did in a year. The attendance is up, and it has been a couple of nights where I thought we were going to run out of booze."

"Well, I'm really just glad that you gave us a chance to even play here. We did a lot of traveling before you gave us a chance, so I just want to thank you for making Marthasville a home for us."

"You are welcome. You know my wife and I were having a conversation about you last night."

"I hope all good things were talked about. I would hate for your wife to not like me."

"No, not that type of conversation, I feel a little funny sharing it with you, but you have done a lot for me and my family in such a short time. I feel as if I need to say something."

"Go ahead and say it, I don't mind."

"Well, it just seems to me that you are doing all of the work here at the saloon. I mean they play instruments for you, and I know that is your husband but what are they really bringing you to the table?"

"What do you mean?"

"Well, since you have been here we have had a packed house every night. But they are not coming to see the men you have with you. They are coming to hear your songs and you play the piano."

"Okay."

"Look out there and tell me what you see."

Carolyn looks out into the saloon and tells him what she sees. "Well, I see a stage and a bar, my husband and the rest of the band."

"Okay, do you know what I see?"

"What?"

"I see an empty bar, a bar that is only full of people when you are performing. You know how much money I pay you to perform every night, right?"

"Yes."
"And you spend more than half of it on feeding, clothing, and a place to sleep for a band that doesn't play a lot of music."

"I don't know if I am following you."

"Look, all I am saying is that you shouldn't be paying someone's way if they aren't helping you at all. You work very hard creating those songs and performing them for our crowds. Hell, I find myself sometimes singing the songs at home, so I know that they are good. But it just doesn't make any darn sense for you to be doing all the work, bringing all the people in here for you to give it right back to me to feed people that aren't doing anything. Even if your husband is one of them."

"I guess I see what you are saying."

"I'm not trying to get in your business or anything. It's just that someone like you with amazing talent, can go very far. Or you can be held back because you are spending time with people that will slow you down. Think about it, will you?" "I will."

Carolyn walks out of the office to see her husband waiting on her with a coat in hand. She walks over to him, and he places the coat on her shoulders before she walks with him outside of the saloon. They walked toward a small diner across the street and go inside to have a late dinner. They go inside and ask for a table. "Dinner for two, please."

"No problem, Mrs. Carolyn. Just give me a minute, and I will clean our best table off for you," said the waiter.

The waiter goes into the dining area of the establishment and cleans the biggest table, located in the middle of the room. He works fast and even asks for assistance from other waiters so that they are not waiting long. As they are seated, the small crowd of people that are still in the restaurant applaud Carolyn as she smiles, says hello and looks over the menu.

"I will have the house special tonight. I love the pot roast you make here. I can't get enough of it."

"I will have the steak and potatoes and apple pie for desert," said her husband.

"You must be hungry."

"A man has to eat. Working every night in the saloon, I have to eat in order to play the piano well."

"We have to get food for the guys to before we leave. They stayed at the hotel because I know you wanted to have dinner alone."

"I'm glad you noticed."

"I have noticed, and since you have been working so hard with coming up with the music and all, I figured you would want some time alone."

"Speaking of songs, we need a new tune to play so that the crowd doesn't get bored. Have you come up with anything since we have gotten here?"

"What do you mean since we got here? Haven't me and the boys been helpful with your shows every night?"

"Yes, you guys have been very helpful with setting up and cleaning the stage but when are you guys going to help with the making of the music is all I am asking."

Carolyn's husband laughs to himself as the food is being delivered to the table. They look over their food and Carolyn begins to eat. Her husband takes his fork and knife and begins to cut his steak. He takes the knife and stabs the piece of meat, looks at his wife and says in the most calming voice, "I remember the first night we performed here in the saloon. We were horrible, everyone that came in to see us quickly walked out of the bar. As we continued to play, I looked over at you and thought about all of the things that I wanted you to have. I remember saying to myself that this is another place that will eventually kick us out and that we would have to go somewhere else to find work. But as long as I had you I would be okay, no matter where we had to go. I was even willing to try to buy a piece of land and maybe work it so that I could finally give you something stable. Then, like if God was listening to my prayers, you got up from where you were, sat at the piano and began to play one of the best songs I have ever heard in my life. Even though I had heard the song once before I couldn't be mad at you because I know why you learned and decided to play it. And it has done very well for us, keeping a roof over our heads and having money to spend. I thought eventually the people would get tired of the same song over and over again, and they did," her husband paused for a second before continuing… "But every time that happened you seemed to come up with a new song, better than the last one you played. So one day when you said that you were going on a horse ride to think of new song lyrics, I decided to follow you and see where you are getting all this inspiration. I was hoping that it was coming from the view of this place. All the mountains and trees give me hope and ideas and I thought it was doing the same for you, and maybe we could have come up with a song together. You know when you started going to that nigger bar I wasn't even mad that you were learning songs from him. It was when I saw you kiss him is when I realized that the fortune and fame mean more to you than our marriage. But even then I figured it wouldn't last long, and that nigger would run out of songs that good clean white folks would want to hear. Well, a week has turned into three months since we came here and you have become the most popular piano player this town has ever had. Hell, people come from other towns and spend lots of money just to see you perform. I wonder what all of those people would think if they knew you were kissing a nigger for songs?"

Carolyn looks up from her plate and says quietly, but with anger, "Look around you and tell me what you see," said Carolyn.

"I see a bunch of people eating their dinner. What does that have to do with anything?" "Well, I see almost everything that you see, except I also see a man that three months ago couldn't buy himself a bath, let alone wash the dirty clothes that he came in here with, and now he sits before me with expensive clothes eating a huge steak that he had no hand in buying. What did you expect of me? Did you think that I would just be okay being with a band that pretends to know how to play instruments? No, so what I did was, I made way for us to have all the things that I wanted us to have. And now that we have all these things you want to complain and worry about me having an affair with some nigger boy that teaches me how to play the piano? You know what else I see, Robert?"

"No, what else do you see?"

"I see a town that loves me and the music that I play for them. They come in after a long hard day at their jobs or in the fields, or just bringing their wife out for a night on the town and listen to my music and go home happy. At the same time, they look at you and the boys and secretly wonder what you guys are actually doing here. Some of them even say that I am wasting my time and want me to just get rid of you. And you know, maybe they are right."

"What do you mean by that?"

"Well, the entire town should know by now how jealous of a man you are. And how easy it would be for you to get jealous and spread lies about me just so that I would lose my job here in town. Why they might just take offense to all of this and throw you and the rest of your flunkies right out of town."

"So what are you saying?"

"I'm saying that I will give you tonight's earnings so that you and your band can move on. I have found a home here in

Marthasville, and I don't think that there will be room for all of us on stage anymore."

"Not even room for your husband?"

Carolyn moves her chair closer to Robert and says to him, "As a husband, you are one of a kind, but as a business partner you are a burden. So, in the morning you and your band should pack up and find a new town to play for. The money from tonight should help you for about three weeks. So you should hurry and find new work. I hear they have been building the railroad back together since the Union army destroyed most of it during the war. I hear the pay is good too. You should run along because you don't have much time."

"And what are you going to do without us?"

"Well, I am going to finish my dinner, and then I am going to go back to the hotel and take a nice long, hot bath. And then I will get into the very expensive bed the hotel's owner purchased for me, and sleep like a baby until the morning. You see they want me to be here, so they take care of me. And when I wake up, hopefully you will be gone, and I can continue to make money. Now off you go, you don't have a lot of time till morning."

Robert throws his napkin onto his unfinished plate and stands up to leave. Just as he rises, the waiter comes back with the food for the rest of the band. He says to Carolyn, "Mrs. Carolyn here is the rest of the food you ordered. I took the liberty of putting it in a picnic basket so it would be easier to carry, but be careful, it's fresh-out the kitchen. So the sides can be a little hot," said the waiter.

"That's wonderful, here is the money for tonight's order. And thank you again. As always you do a perfect job."
"Thank you, Mrs. Carolyn, but your money is no good here. The owner goes out and sees your show every other night. It is our honor to serve you in our kitchen."

"That is very thoughtful of him to do. Tell him the next time he comes over I will play a special song for him and his wife."

"I will, and if it is not a bother, could you sign this napkin for my wife? She really loves your music also."

"Of course I will. If it wasn't for people like you I wouldn't be here."

Carolyn signs the napkin as Robert looks on in anger. She takes the money she was given back and the money inside of her purse and puts it into the picnic basket that holds the food for the band members. Robert picks up the basket quickly and starts to walk out of the restaurant.

"I hope everything you need is in the basket, Mr. You know, all this time you two have been here in Marthasville I never asked your name."

"It's Robert. Don't worry about it. I will be leaving in the morning anyway."

"Really?! Mrs. Carolyn, you never mentioned that you were leaving, what will we do without you here to sing for us?"

"I am not leaving, my band is. They feel I have been holding them back because we usually don't stay in a town this long, so they are going to move on. I don't know what I will do without them."

"Well, it's been a pleasure serving you as well. I hope that you and your band find success where-ever you go."

"We will, as long as we can write songs and play music there will always be somewhere for us to go. I hear there are a couple of saloons north of here that pay very well for good music. I think we will visit them."

Robert walks out of the restaurant as Carolyn finishes up her dinner.

The next morning Robert and the rest of the band did just as Carolyn had requested. They packed their belongings and left the town, only leaving a note for Carolyn that she picked up later from the front desk of the hotel. Carolyn leaves her room as she does every morning for breakfast. When she gets into the lobby of the hotel the man at the desk calls for her attention.

"Mrs. Carolyn may I please speak to you for a moment," said the desk clerk. "Yes, of course, what can I do for you?"

"I don't mean to bother you, but I have a letter here from your husband. He left it here when they left this morning, wanted me to give it to you as soon as I saw you."

"Thank you very much for remembering."

Carolyn opens and reads the letter to herself.

Dear Love,

It has finally come to a point where we can no longer be in each other's lives. You have finally achieved the dream that we both set out for when we left that small town in Virginia, and I can not tell you how proud I am of you. One day you will see that you

will need me again, and until then I will go on and find work.
There are plenty of saloon's that would love to hear us play.

Until you come back to me,

"I hope that everything is okay, Ma'am."

"Oh yes, just my husband writing me a letter saying how much he loves me. He wants me to meet him in the town that they are going to, but I have found such-a home here."

"Yes, Mrs. Carolyn we would hate to lose you. What ever would we do without your music here in town?"

"You know since you put it that way I think I will stay. I think I will be having breakfast this morning. You think they are still serving at this time of day?"

"For you, Mrs. Carolyn, I think they will make an exception."

At that time, Nathan is standing inside of Mrs. Debbie's bar cleaning and making up a new song. He is standing with his back to the door sweeping the floor and dancing when he thinks of a new lyric he stops and writes it down on a small piece of paper.

Robert and his friends walk-in as Mrs. Debbie watches them go toward Robert. She grabs her shotgun from the back of the bar and raises it toward them and says, "What the hell do you want here? I have paid the money already for the month so you shouldn't be here."

"Well, as much as I like this place I am not here to take anything of yours. We are here for Nathan."

Nathan and Mrs. Debbie look at each other with a puzzled look as Robert keeps talking.

"You know who I am, right?"

"Never seen you before in my life."

"Well, I wasn't talking to you now, was I? No, I was talking to him. Now, you know who I am right, Nathan?"

"I think that you are Mrs. Carolyn's husband, right?"

Robert continues to walk around the bar, lifting and looking and glasses on the tables' and taking drinks of-the-alcohol behind the bar.

"That's right, I am glad that you have been paying attention, seeing as my wife has been seeing you for the past three months. Coming all the way out here to the nigger part of town, she must really like you."

Mrs. Debbie is now looking at Nathan with anger in her eyes. She told Nathan from the first day Carolyn came into the bar, that she was trouble, but he did not listen. She lowers her gun and continues to let Robert talk.

"I don't know what you mean, sir. Yes, Mrs. Carolyn was coming here once a week to learn how to play the piano, but I would never disrespect you or her by trying something unspeakable."

"Unspeakable? Well, I will say it then. You were trying to fuck my wife weren't you?"

"No, sir. Not at all."

"Then tell me, boy. What would she be doing all the way out here visiting you if you weren't trying to have sex with her?"

"She would come out here and ask me to teach her how to play the piano." "Piano? Now tell me, little nigger, why would a renowned piano player need you to teach her how to play?"

"Well, when she got here she didn't really know how to play. She asked if I would teach her a couple of songs and I did, that was all."

"And in return what did she give you?"

"She gave me nothing, sir."

"Well, because of you she doesn't need us anymore. She says because of you and your help she can make more money on her own, than staying with us. Did you know she was playing your songs for the good white folk in town?"

"No, sir, I didn't know that."

"And now she has become a solo act."

"I am sorry to hear that, sir. I wish there was something that I could do for you."

"Well, I am glad you said that because my partners and I thought this was going to go a lot differently."

"What do you mean, sir?"

"Well, since you are the reason we are out of a job we were just going to come down here and start shooting. You and the lovely lady with the shotgun behind the counter would have been found dead so that she could never come a get another song from you again. But, on the way here I thought of something much better."

"And that would be, sir?"

"You come with us so that no one has to die. We know how important this hole in the wall is to your kind and we would hate for it to shut down because we had to kill that fat bitch."

"What did you say?"

"Mrs. Debbie, please hush, I will come with you guys so that there will be no more trouble."

That's a good nigger. Now, get only what you have here in the bar and let's go. We have a lot of ground to cover, and we gotta get moving.

Mrs. Debbie goes to raise the gun she has in her hands, and Nathan puts his palm on the barrel and pushes it to the floor. He turns to her and says in a low and stern voice.

"I do not want you to get hurt by these men because we didn't listen to what they are saying. I caused this, and I am going to do what is best for the both of us."

"They will kill you. Child don't you understand that? They will take you from here, and if they don't kill you, they will make you wish you were dead."

"I know that, but I was the one that didn't listen when you told me she was bad for me. I thought that she would be able to take me out of here with the music I was showing her how to play, and instead, I am going to get killed for it."

"Now you listen to me, whatever you do you make sure you keep your chin up. If they see you getting down about all of this eventually, they will see that they don't need you anymore."

"I know that, and I also know that they are not a great band. They are going to need me so that they can make money. Just remember these words and when we leave here the first thing you need to do is go and tell Mark what has happened."

"Okay, what are the words?"

"The days we spend

The times we share

All alone at this piano

Wishing you were there

But through it all, I sing out loud

Knowing that you are listening

And hope that you are proud."

"What does that mean?"

"It's a song, it's one of my best songs and if they are going to make me play the piano that is the song I will sing. Just make sure you tell Mark the song so that if they are able to come looking for me, they will know how to find me. Now, repeat it back to me, Mrs. Debbie."

"The days we spend

The times we share

All alone at this piano

Wishing you were there

But through it all, I sing out loud

Knowing that you are listening

And *hope that you are proud."*

"I love you, Mrs. Debbie. Now just stay-in here until we are gone."

"I will, and I will hurry and tell Mark about what has happened."

"Okay, I will be okay. Just don't forget the song."

"I won't."

Nathan walks out of the bar where Robert and the rest of the men are waiting on horseback. Robert walks over to the carriage on the lead horse, and Robert says, "There is no reason for you to ride in the carriage, I have nothing more to say. Let's just tie you to the back of the wagon, that way when people see us they know that you are just another nigger. And just so you know."

Robert smacks Nathan in the face sending him to the ground.

"That is the beginning to what is going to happen to you because you slept with my wife."

Robert ties Nathan's hands to the back of the wagon with a long rope, and they head north in search of work. Nathan looks back and sees Mrs. Debbie peeking out of the front door waiting for them to be out of sight so she can go tell Mark. She runs as fast as she can across the small town trying to control herself from crying. She runs out of breath for a moment and leans on a tree not to far from the twins home. She finally reaches the house screaming as loud as she can as she gets closer to the door for the twins to come out. Meanwhile, inside the house, the twins are cleaning with their father. Mark finally hears Mrs. Debbie's cry for help and runs toward the door, and his brother shortly follows him.

"Ms. Debbie, what is wrong? Why are you making such a fuss out here?"

"They got Nathan, baby they gone kill him."

"Who has Nathan?"

"The man that is married to that new singer in town."

"Mrs. Carolyn? Why would her husband kidnap Nathan?"

Mrs. Debbie goes on to tell the story to the twins of how Nathan and Mrs. Carolyn were meeting so that she could learn to play the piano better. She tells them that for the last three months she has been visiting without her knowledge. And that Nathan has been giving her songs to play in town at the saloon. The twins are shocked at what they hear, and Matthew says to the both of them.

"I think that we should go over to see the new sheriff, maybe he will be able to help us go get him."

"Why would he help us? All he is there for is to go and tell Sheriff Thomas what we are doing out here. We need to leave now and go get him ourselves."

"And what are we going to do when we find him?" "We are going to bring him back, however we need to."

"Yea, and then we end up in jail because five or more white men say that we stole from them. No, we are going to the sheriff."

Mark walks away from Matthew so that he can collect his thoughts. He returns and says to him, "We will go to the sheriff so that he can tell us there is nothing he can do. And after we do that we are going to go get him ourselves. Now I am willing to try it your way, even though I know that it will not work, but I need you to promise me that you will help me if I am right."

"I promise, but why are you so concerned about helping him?"

"Because he is my friend, and if we as a People don't help each other how do we expect to be treated the same by people that don't look like us?"

Without a word, Matthew and Mark walk with Mrs. Debbie to the sheriff's office. They walk into the new jail Walter and Elijah have built, and it is empty, they turn and see the light on in the church and go there. Inside the newly built and empty church are Walter and Elijah having dinner sitting on small boxes with a candle in between the two of them.

"Mr. Sheriff we need your help."

"What can I do for you two boys, and also you ma'am?"

"One of your friends has been taken against their wishes. And we believe that if we don't do something soon, he will be killed." "Okay, son what is your friend's name?"

"Nathan. Nathan Washington."

"The boy who plays the piano down at Mrs. Debbie's?"

"Yes they took him away, and we have to do something to get him back." "Okay son, just tell me what you know."

Matthew begins to tell the story to Walter and Elijah as they listen intently to every word he is saying. Matthew finishes and Walter says to him, "I think that we need to go see the sheriff in town and see what he says about it."

Mark looks at Matthew and says, "What did I tell you was going to happen? Let's just do it ourselves because we are wasting a lot of time!"

"No, I said I will follow you only if my way doesn't work and now we are going to the sheriff."

Walter looks over at Elijah and says to him, "I am going to take the boys over to town to talk to the sheriff. I need you to stay here and look after Mrs. Debbie until we get back."

Walter and the twins leave the church headed toward the town. As they walk Mark starts to become impatient knowing there will be nothing done.

"You two do know that we are wasting time, the only thing the sheriff will do is tell us thank you for telling him about the problem and nothing will be done."

"Well, I have talked to the sheriff myself, and he has said any problems they will address them."

Walter and the twins walk into the town with all eyes on them. They barely make it to the street before someone runs over to the sheriff's office to tell him that they are coming. Everyone in the town that can see is gazing at the three men as if they are bringing in a horrible plague. Before they can get to the sheriff, he comes running out of his office with Festus and meets them in the middle of the town. Sheriff Thomas still wearing a napkin tucked in his shirt from eating turns them around and starts to walk back out of the town and says, "We didn't expect to see you this early on, Walter. What seems to be the problem?"

"Well, we seem to have a kidnapping of a boy in our area."
"Well, who did they take? And who took him?"

"Nathan Washington is the boy's name, and it just happened about two hours ago. Enough time for you to catch up to them and bring him back."

"Okay, so who did the kidnapping?"

"Well, they say the new lady in town, you know the one that sings at the saloon.

Her husband was the one that took Nathan."
"And why would they do that?"

Walter looks at the twins and thinks long and hard about what he is going to tell the sheriff. He knows that if he tells them the truth they would not believe him. They would also be very upset that he was talking bad or telling lies about Mrs. Carolyn and something even worse may happen.

"Well, I'm not quite sure why they would take him."

"Then you are wasting our time. And the fact that what you are saying may get you in more trouble then you could imagine. I think that you three should just keep walking toward your homes and forget about it. We will keep an eye out for Nathan, maybe he ran away or something."

"Yea, maybe he ran away."

Sheriff Thomas takes the napkin out of his shirt and says, "Now, I am going back to my dinner, which is probably cold by now because of all this mess."

Sheriff Thomas turns and starts to walk toward the town. Festus turns to them and says, "Do me a favor? The next time you have a problem like this try to figure it out in your own town. Sheriff Thomas has enough trouble keeping up with the problems of good respectable white folks here in town. He doesn't have time to try to figure out all the mess and problem you nigger's got down there on your end, do you understand?"

"Yes, we understand."

Festus walks away leaving Walter and the twins to their thoughts. Walter looks at the twins and says to them.

"Well, I guess that is all we can do for now."

"What do you mean? They just told us they weren't going to do anything." "Which is exactly what I told you would happen! Now, it's time for my idea." Mark walks away from the two men toward their town. Matthew turns to Walter and says "Thank you for trying to help us."

"Sorry I couldn't do more, but my hands are tied. Why is your brother so mad?" Matthew turns in the direction of his brother and says, "I think he is mad because he is realizing that the only way to help is to help ourselves."

"And what does that mean?"

Matthew starts to walk in the direction of his brother and says, "Ask the Indians." Matthew catches up to his brother just before they go into their father's home.

Mark stops his brother just before he goes in the front door and says, "So what are we going to tell our father? I mean we can't tell him what we are really going to do, can we?"

"We don't have time for lies. We have to tell him the truth and get out of here as fast as possible."
Mark and Matthew walk into their home and talk to their father over dinner. As they explain everything that has been going on, John sits in disbelief. How were they even approached about the situation? How did Nathan even know the lady he has slept with? And why would they take him away? Finally, after they finished telling the story to their father, he drops the fork he was using on the plate in front of him. He gets up and starts to clean off the plates by scraping off the leftovers outside of the house. He goes back into the house and pours warmed water from the fire into a bucket to clean the plates. He stands and cleans

quietly for a while when Mark says to him, "So, what do you think of all of this, Pa?"

"You know, when I was your age, I had a friend that was taken the same way. See, he belonged to a farmer that was very easy on his slaves. Hell, they only worked five to eight hours a day and were dressed very well. They were treated like kings and queens on that plantation with their owner being a doctor as well. He would even show me how to read during the evenings. He said that a man that couldn't read is like a lion that can't see or smell. And every night he would read to some of us so that we would at least know how to read a sign if we were freed. Till one day they were told that their owner had passed away. He had a weak heart and one morning it didn't beat strong enough for him to wake up. Well, seeing is that the doctor never married and had no children, his sister had to come and sell all of his belongings, including his slaves. She was upset that they were treated so well and told her brother often about her disapproval of it. She said that his niggers were no better than the hogs he had on his property and treating them well only

235

made them think that they were regular people," he paused for a moment before continuing.

"So, the first thing she did was have an auction for all the cattle and niggers on the plantation. I can still remember the poster sign on the wall of the supply store saying that the auction was to be held that Saturday and everything must go, even at a low cost. Well, my friend was a house nigger. He never spent a day in the fields, and the day of the auction he was sold to a man that was growing cotton in Mississippi. The man took him back to his plantation and made him pick cotton from sun up to sun down for the first week until he was so tired he couldn't move anymore. So the man whipped him dead like he was a lame horse, said that no nigger ever took a break on his farm and it wasn't going to start then. I was about 12 years old when I had finally heard the news, and to this day I wish that I could have done something to help him so that maybe he would be alive today. But I was scared, and anyone I would tell about my plan would tell me that I was crazy and looking to be hung. I have always been proud of you two for sticking up for each other no matter how big the problem is, so I want you to go and find your friend. I want you to do all of the things that I was taught couldn't happen. Go find your friend, sons. Just promise me that you will look out for each other and return safely."

"We will, Pa."

"You know, there is a new church at the end of town. Haven't been to church in awhile. I think I will go in the morning."

Chapter 12

That next morning the twins got up and out of the house as early as they could so that they wouldn't fall too far behind Robert and his band. Because of Debbie they knew what direction to go into, but had no idea where to start looking. As they start their journey, their father goes and visits Elijah's church for the first time. This is the first Sunday that Elijah has preached in this town and a lot of people have come out to hear him. John walks into the church just as Elijah is starting to speak.

"This morning I want to talk about faith, I am talking about real faith. See, it is easy to have faith in something you know will happen eventually. Maybe not in the time you would like it to happen, but you know eventually if you work hard enough it will start to work in your favor. No, I am talking about the kind of faith you have-to-have when things don't look like they will ever turn around. When I was a boy, there was this woman who lived with her husband not too far from the plantation I lived on. The husband was a traveling merchant who got word from the far west that he could make a lot of money with the things he was selling if he would pack up and move there. So the man packed what he had and told his wife that he would return one day with more money than she could count. And to pray for him every day until he returned so they could live the life they had always wanted. Well, three years had come and gone, and there was no sign of her husband. Some people in town even started to talk and try to convince her that she needed to move on with her life and forget about him, but she just kept praying. She was an attractive woman, and all the men in town rich to poor tried to get her to forget him and marry them, promising everything under the sun, but she just kept praying. The farm they owned was run down, and all the cattle they once owned was dead or had to be sold to make it to the next day, but she just kept praying. She finally had to sell the farm because there was nothing else to sell and even though it hurt her heart she just kept praying for her husband to make it back home. She even had to get a job working as a maid for a woman she knew, so that she could make a little money, but she got up every day and praised God for the chance to show her faith. And no matter what happened or what anyone said, she kept praying and never felt sorry for herself, giving all praise and glory to God. Until one day, when she was on her last of the last she looked up into the sky and thanked God one more time, and before her eyes could get back to the ground in the distance, her husband was walking toward her limping from the hills. Turns out he had broken his leg in Indian territory, and they helped him back to health. And he had done everything that he had promised his wife, and they lived out their lives receiving and giving all the blessings God allowed them to be a part of. John 15:5 talks about God being the vine and us as his people, being the branches, and those that remain loyal to him will receive bountiful fruit or blessings, if they stay with him. I know you all have faith, but my question to you is for how long? How long will you hold on to God without being distracted by what happens to you or what people think of you? We all have to understand that what we want in our time and what God wants for us in his time are two different things. And the longer you believe in what God has in store, the more fruitful your blessings will be."

Mark and Matthew walk for a moment before they start to talk to each other. Mark is focused on finding his friend before something bad happens to him. Matthew is concerned about his brother and his temper. He knows that Mark can jump the gun sometimes and he couldn't live with himself if something was to happen to him. In the distance is the lake and forest that they have been training in for the past three months. Standing as if he has been waiting on the twins is Emmet and the old lady they had followed when they first met him. They walk up to them, and Mark begins to talk.

"Look, I know you want us to be here and be ready for the mission you have planned for us, but we have to leave. Our friend was taken away by some white men, and we need to catch up to them before it's too late."

"I know, I was waiting here for you two so that I could say some things before you left. And to offer some help."

"Well, what is it that you have to say?"

"There are three rules to follow when on a mission like this one. The first is to only travel at night, it is getting cold outside, and most people are in their homes after the sun goes down. That allows you to move freely on the outskirts of towns and gives you a chance to go inside of towns without being seen. Second, when in need always use what is around you, grass, rocks, and trees can all be used to hide from people that will not be nice to you. Some of them will even return you to slavery in other states if you are not careful. And lastly, never trust anyone other than the people you are leaving here with. When to many people are involved it leaves room for more people to find out."

"People? It's just Mark and I."

"I have also asked Minty to go with you during your time away."

"Why would we want some old lady with us? She will do nothing but slow us down."

"Minty is very resourceful and knows her way from here all the way to Canada. She has made the journey many of times being one of the first people to be recruited by this organization."

"We can tell! How old is she?"
"No one really knows how old she is. But she fought for our people since she can remember and that is good enough for me. I will be sending messages ahead of you to tell you what I have learned after today."

"How will we get them?"

"They will find you. And lastly here are a couple of things George has given me to give to you for your journey. Do you remember that machine that made the rubber?"

"Yes."

"Well, he has made some type of shoe for you to try out. He says they will allow you to run faster in the forest and climb trees better. He also gave you two a pair of jackets that you helped him test out at headquarters."

"How can I forget that."

"Well, he also wanted me to tell you that you only get one shot with these jackets. If you get hit more than once there is a chance the jacket will not work, and you could die. And lastly, he told me to give you two this."

Emmet gives Matthew a small and weird looking cloth with a stand. The twins look at Emmet with a puzzled look, and Matthew says, "What is this?"

"It's a light director for your fires at night. If you put this up behind the back of the fire, the light from the flames won't be seen by people in the neighboring towns. The cloth is fire resistant and directs the light on only what you want to see. That way you can stay warm without anyone noticing you. Be careful you two and when you get back be ready for another mission."

"We will, and thank you for helping us."

"If we don't help ourselves, then who will?"

Just as Emmet finishes talking, Mrs. Debbie is riding in on her horse and carriage toward them. She yells out for the twins to get their attention. They look and then turn back to Emmet who is not standing there anymore. Mrs. Debbie catches up to the twins and says to them.

"I almost forgot to tell you, before Nathan was taken away he told me to remember something to say to you."

"What was that?"

"I'm not really sure. It sounded like some song he was working on, and he said that it would help you."

"So what did he say?"

"The days we spend."

The times we share

All alone at this piano

Wishing you were there

But through it all I sing out loud

Knowing that you are listening

And hope that you are proud."

"What does that mean?"

"Look, he just told me to tell it to you before he was gone. I was so upset yesterday that I forgot to tell you. Please bring that boy back home, he is not my child, but I love him as if he was my own son. Just be careful you two. The world is not too kind to people like us."

"We will, Mrs. Debbie you go back home now."

Mrs. Debbie turns her carriage around and goes back toward the town. The boys turn back around and there in the shadows stands Emmet waiting.

"You sure know how to disappear when you need too."

"It is the reason I am still alive. Maybe you should pay attention, those shoes really work when trying to hide in the trees. I got word from Marionville saying that Nathan and his kidnappers are on the way there. Apparently, they have booked Nathan in a whites only saloon to play his music."

"Thanks for the equipment and the direction to go in."

"No problem, just make it back safe."

The twins start their journey toward Marionville as-Emmet watches them leave.

Minty stays back to have a few words with Emmet about all that is going on.

"I don't understand why I have to go with them."

"I need you to look after them while they are looking for their friend. This is a simple mission for them, and it is very important that they come back in one piece. That is why I need your help, Minty. You are the best agent we have, and I know you will make sure they return."

"I will, but I think this may be my last mission."

"Are you sure?"

"Yes, I mean it this time. I am an old woman, and it's time for me to rest and let some youngster do this. I think I have earned my right to retire. I just don't get why you want to help them so much."

"Well, since their uncle died under my command I feel that I owe them."

"Well, as always I will do my best. But, I didn't come this far to die for some kids, so if they don't listen I will shoot them."

"I know, Minty. Thank you for going with them."

"You are welcome, just don't ask me anymore after this, I am done." "I know, before you leave, I want to give you this."

Emmet goes into his coat pocket and pulls out a small map.

"What is it?"

"Do you remember the story of John Henry?"

"Is that the big strong colored boy from Virginia? Wasn't he the one that challenged that steam engine to see who could get through the mountain the fastest?"

"That's the man."

"I thought he died years ago? And what good is he going to do us? We are not laying any railroad."

"He did, but most people don't know that before he went and worked for the railway, he dug tunnels all over the coast. Here is a map he had given his son right before he died, it shows all of the tunnels he dug over the years. Some of them are almost 100 miles or more underground. You can use them if they are still there to move a little faster without being seen."

"I thought that story was just a made-up story?"

"No, it was actually true. Most stories of negroes doing great things are turned into folklore. God forbid us to think for a moment that we can do great things without the help of the people who brought us here. We may begin to think that we can govern ourselves."

"You know I can't read this."

"I do, but the twins know how to read. I do know that with it being in your hands nothing bad will happen to it. If it gets into the wrong hands, there is no telling what will happen. Be safe, Minty."

"I will. And just so you know I am talking them to see Mrs. Darlene."

"You know they are not going to want to do that."

"Then they are not going to get my help. You know I have never left from this area without seeing her, and I am not going to start now!"

"I understand, but I ain't going with you now am I?"

"No, you are not, but if they are going to be with me, they are going to follow my rules."

"I couldn't agree with you more, Minty."

"Don't be a smart-ass."

"No, ma'am. Not at all."

Minty looks at Emmet with a very stern look and starts to follow the twins on their journey. Just then George comes limping from behind Emmet and nearly scares him.

"For goodness sakes, George. You almost made me kill you. What are you doing out here anyway?"

"Getting some fresh air. You taught me how to stay in the shadows and not want me to use them? So, what do you think?"

"About what?"

"About Minty going with the boys? You know she doesn't like going out with younger people, she always says that they are too hot-headed and pigheaded to ever get passed North Carolina."

"To be honest I am a little nervous about it. I know that Minty will do all she can, but I hope that the boys don't get distracted by the fact that it's their friend."

"Then why did you let them go?"

"Because they needed to be tested, and no human could have come up with a better one for them."

"I understand."

"Wish I had some tobacco."

"I don't have any loose tobacco, but I do have one of these to share."

George goes into his lab coat pocket and pulls out what looks to be a pre-rolled cigarette. He gives it to Emmet and lights it for him.

"What is this?"

"It's a cigarette."

Emmet takes a drag from the cigarette and is truly impressed by the taste of it. It shows as he licks his lips in delight.

"What is that remarkable taste?"

"You know how when you smoke cigarettes there is always that dark tar at the end?"

"Yes."

"Well, I took a piece of cotton and soaked it in water filled with mint leaves. Let it dry and used it to extend the cigarette from my lips. Not only did it stop the tar from getting on my lips but it actually trapped it inside. I haven't come up with a name for it yet, but I think I am on to something."

"Yes, you are! Can I have some more of them?"

"Well, I have to make them, seeing that the one you are holding is the only one I have at this moment."

George and Emmet look at each other for a moment, and finally, both look down at the cigarette. Emmet hands the cigarette to George.

"Thank you. I said share not have. I'll make you up a couple when we get back."

"Thank you."

Chapter 13

(October 25, 1897) - Elijah and Walter

"I talk with a friend."

The next day after service was a cooler day here in Marthasville. The day was still warm and sunny, but there seemed to be a cool breeze that blows through our town every couple of minutes. I got up early to start on the construction of the church. I helped Walter with his work on the property. So today starts the construction of the church. Walter gets up at his regular time and meets me in the morning for breakfast. It was my turn to cook so he must have smelled it from all the way over at his place.

"Good morning, preacher!"

"Good morning, Elijah. I hope you slept well last night."

"I did, and after that beautiful sermon you gave I feel rested and full from the word."

"Well, I thank you. That means I did my job."

"Yes, you did. I do have a couple of questions about the sermon this morning if you don't mind."

"That's fine with me, I am getting the food out of the skillet now."

Walter goes into the dining area where the plates are already set to eat. Elijah walks into the room from the kitchen and serves the food. He takes the skillet back into the kitchen and finally sits down at the table.

"Looks good."

"I hope it is good. So what is it that you have on your mind?"

"It can wait 'til after breakfast. I don't want to interrupt your breakfast with all my questions."

"Well, I think that it makes for good breakfast when you have early morning conversations. Gets the brain going."

"That's true. Well, I think the only real question I have is why is God so forgiving?"

"What do you mean?"

"Well, I can remember as a boy when I was in Texas how when old Mr. Pennington would talk about God and that he was a vengeful and quick to anger God who punished anyone of us for stepping out of line. I can remember a time when the crops didn't come back exactly as the old man had predicted and because of that, he blamed us. He constantly whipped us for the fact that it hadn't rained in Texas for about a month. And, because he felt that it was our evil ways that made God mad he stopped feeding us so that he could make a profit with the food that had grown."

"Really?"

"Yes, that's what happened. But you know what? Ever since they let us be free and letting us preach our own way the story about God has changed. He is forgiving and slow to anger, he turns the other cheek and looks down on violence toward man. I guess my question is, are there two Gods? And we just ended up with the one that doesn't use violence as a control tool?"

"Well, I think what happened is people weren't able to read back then."

"I don't understand?"

"Well, it was a law not too long ago saying that if any of us were caught reading and writing there would be punishment. Right?"

"Yes."

"Well, my Poppa always use to tell my brothers and I that the only way we would really know what God wanted us to do is to read his book word-for-word. A lot of times the white man skips over chapters of the bible, only to read a couple of verses to make a point. And I reckon that with any book, if you do the same things you can make a fuss about whatever you want or don't want. Have you ever read the bible, all the way through, Walter?"

"No, I haven't."

"You should. It talks about compassionate God, one that loves his creations, but isn't happy with their choices. And just like anyone else on this earth, he praises the good and rebukes the bad. But, then, later on, it talks about his Son who was sent down to the earth to forgive us of our sins. Now, when God does this he sends us someone who is very compassionate, but only for those people that didn't know any better."

"I don't understand."

"Well, Jesus in the bible had compassion for the misguided. He actually spent most of his time trying to show the people they were being led down the wrong path. Even his disciples were tax collectors before they met him. And I'm not talking about the kind we have now that will come and close your farm down because you didn't pay taxes. I'm talking about the kind that beat your kids up until you came up with the money. But through all of that, Jesus kept a level head, that is until he ran into the people that should have known better."

There is a part in the bible where Jesus loses his temper because he witnesses people making a profit in a place designed for his father. He loses it and destroys most of the merchant property that was being displayed in the tabernacle. Which tells me that the holiest man to ever walk God's green earth had a temper, it just took a lot more to get to, than the average man.

"So what are you trying to say?"

"That if Jesus himself being the son of God had a limit to what he was willing to accept, then you and I have that same choice. So, in the end, it really is about what we will and will not tolerate."

Walter continues to look at Elijah eat his food as he thinks about what he has just heard. Elijah finally realizing he is being watched, looks up at Walter and says, "Eat your food while it is hot, son. When it is fresh, it is good for you and full of flavor. But, if you leave it to get cold, it will lose its taste. That's when people try to put their own spices on things to make it to their own liking."

Walter looks down at his food and then smiles at Elijah and says, "You're right, I understand now."

Walter and Elijah finish their breakfast in silence.

(November 1, 1897) - "Going to see Mrs. Darlene."

Mark and Matthew have been walking for days now, trying to catch up to their friend, Nathan and his kidnappers. They have been following the rules Emmet has given them to the letter, staying away from all main roads and traveling mostly at nightfall when people were retiring to their homes.

During the day they are taking a much-needed rest in the deep part of the forest where no one can see them. As they take shifts sleeping and keeping watch Matthew asks Minty a question about how it all started. As she lays there on the ground, Matthew asks, "Minty, may I ask you a question?"

"Sure, just keep your voice down."

"Yes, ma'am. Well, I want to thank you first for coming with us to find our friend."

"You're welcome. Now, what is the problem?"

"Well, it's not really a problem. I just wanted to know how all this came about? I mean how did all of this happen without any white people finding out?"

"Well, it happened about 200 years ago when they started to bring slaves over from our home, Africa. See, in the white man's books, he would have you believe that all the negroes that were brought here were obedient and passive. But the truth is that some of the boats that were bringing slaves over were taken back by the Africans on board, and because they were closer to American than Africa they decided to come here. Now, what they would have you believe is that white people invented boats and direction, which is not true at all. The Africans that you and I come from began mapping out the stars and sailing way before Christopher Columbus was born. So when our ancestors took over these different ships, they knew exactly how to use them. And instead of going into the ports in Virginia and the Carolina's they sailed into Florida, which was run by the Indians who were pushed out during the war. They accepted us, and in exchange for the boats, they taught us how to farm and defend ourselves in their native ways. Hand-to-hand combat, riding horses, and using the land for food. And when the time was right they sent us on our way with one mission in mind."

"And what was that?"

"To free our people from what we had done to ourselves. The only reason we became slaves is because we allowed the whites to come into our country and take us without any resistance. So, it is only up to us to change that by doing what you are trying to do for your friend."

"And what is that?"

"To free him from injustice and get him to safety."

Just then Mark wakes up and says, "Well, I have one last question then."

"And what is that?"

"Were you one of the original slaves off the boat?"

Minty turns to Matthew and says, "Did I tell you that your brother is the reason I didn't want to come with you two?"

"And why is that?"
"Because you are hard-headed and you think you are funny. And I don't like people like that, especially kids."

"And why is that?"

"Because those are the ones that get killed the fastest. So there is no reason to like them because they won't be around that long."

"So what are you saying, that I won't make it?"

"I'm saying that if you are like any of the other ones I tried to help, then you won't be. And since you bring it up, I want to tell the both of you that we will be going to visit a close friend of mine first before we go after your friend."

Matthew

Why are we going there first?

"Because before every mission I have been sent on for the last 30 years, I have visited this lady so that I do not make any mistakes. She is an Indian spirit woman and her outlook on anything you or I do is very valuable."

"Well, I think we will be wasting time if we go and see her. If we just stay on course, we can reach Nathan and that white man before they even reach the next town."

"Like I said I am going to see Ms. Darlene before I do anything. So, if you want to go on by yourself, it's fine with me. Just remember what I told you about those that don't listen."

Matthew and Mark look over at each other as Minty eats a piece of dry meat. She looks up at the both of them waiting for a response until when Matthew starts to speak.

"We will be going with you to visit your friend first. I just hope that it doesn't stop us from reaching Nathan before he is killed."

"Don't worry, if they were going to kill him we would have found his body or parts of it by now."

Minty finishes her food and then lays down in the high grass to sleep for a moment. Matthew and Mark do the same for a couple of moments looking up at the sky, until Mark asks Minty a question.

"Minty."

"Yes."

"Why do you think they would have killed him by now if they didn't need him for something?"

Minty sits up and takes her straw hat from her face and says, "You should ask the Indians."

Minty slaps the dust off of her hat on her dress, puts it back on her face and lays back down.

They sleep most of the day and start back traveling as the sun falls. They travel some time before they reached a small town in the middle of a dense forest. The town only has three buildings, one being a store and the other two for housing.

The sun is starting to rise as they reach the town and Minty seems to be getting excited to be there. She starts to walk a little faster as the village gets closer, so the twins do the same. Just as they get to the tree line that opens up to the village three small children stand waiting with squirrel guns pointed at their heads.

Minty continues to walk into the village as the children stand in front of the two men. One of the children finally says, "You here with Ms. Minty?"

"Yes."

"Then what is here real name?"

"We don't know. She told us to call her Minty, so that's what we call her." A second child cocks back the hammer of a rifle and points it at the back of Mark's head. They walk them into the village were Minty is hugging a woman as if she has not seen her in a long time.

The lady is a heavier woman with fair skin. She is dressed in Indian clothing and smokes a pipe made of wood and corn husk. They talk to each other in Black Foot Indian, which takes the twins by surprise, because the language is familiar to them yet they don't know where they may have learned it. "Hello, you two. How was the trip from Marthasville?"

"It was a long walk, but peaceful. Well, that is until we got here, now I don't know if my head will be blown off by this rifle in the back of it."

Matthew looks at his brother in amazement because he speaks the language back to Ms. Darlene as if he has used it all his life. Mark looks over at Matthew and says, "What?"

"Do you know you are talking in a different language?"

"No."

The children that are holding guns to the twins all of a sudden take them away and run off starting to play before they start their daily chores. Minty and Ms. Darlene both laugh at the twins as Matthew says, "What's so funny?"

"You do realize both of you are talking in Siksika, right?"

"What's that?"

"It's the native language of the Blackfoot Indian, you and your brother are talking to each other in it right now."
"We are?"

"Yes, you are, and it sounds wonderful. You two come on over to the house so that you can eat. I know you have questions you need answered and a lot of ground to cover before you get where you are going."

They all go into one of the houses and get ready for breakfast. Minty and the twins go down to a small lake located close to the house so that they all bathe in while Ms. Darlene prepares breakfast for everyone. The children run down the small river with fresh clothes, while the clothes they had been wearing are being washed by other children. They all finish cleaning up and head for the house to eat breakfast with Ms. Darlene.

Once back at the home they all sit down with what seems to be over 15 children and all hold hands in prayer. Ms. Darlene goes on to say in her prayer, "Lord, I want to thank you for bringing my good friend and her companions in safely this morning, so that they can come and have food with us and catch up on old times. I want to thank you also for providing for us day in and out with the things that we need to survive. Please watch over us all as we fight the good fight and try to live in your favor. In Jesus name, Amen."

The entire table says amen as the children begin to make plates for everyone.

They begin to eat in silence, and then all of a sudden Matthew starts to talk.

"You know, I always thought my brother and I just had a different bond than most. My aunt would say that Mark and I had made up our own language that only we could understand and that we eventually would grow out of it. The funny part is we did. I can't remember the last time we talked to each other like that before today. And know to find out that it is actually a language, makes me think about what else we know that we have taken for granted."

"You weren't taking it for granted, Matthew. You were being prepared for something long before you could understand why. Your uncle used to speak like that to you two as often as he could, and eventually, you picked it up and started using it when you were in trouble, or saying something you weren't supposed to."

"How do you know that?"

"Because she was watching you. She has been since the day your mother had you two."

"Is that true, Minty?"

"Yes it is, just like these little ones are being raised for the bettering of our people so were you, you just didn't know as much at an early age like these two did."

"Well, why is that?"

"Because it was your mother's choice to raise you in hopes of making you a part of the cause, not your fathers. So for years your mother and uncle taught you in secret hoping no one would find out before you could defend yourselves."

"So, what are you saying? My father didn't want us to be apart of this?"

"I think what she is saying is that your father wasn't comfortable with what could have happened if someone was to find out like so many others who never got a chance to go into action."

Minty looks at Ms. Darlene and says, "Yea, that's what I mean. Ms. Darlene, I want to thank you for this lovely breakfast but do you mind if I excuse myself?"

"Not at all, friend. I know that you are tired so do as you wish."

Minty leaves the table and walks toward the lake. The twins look at each other puzzled at why Minty was so angry at the table. Ms. Darlene seeing that the boys have no clue on what has happened in the past she starts to explain Minty and why she is the way she is.

"You know, you two I have known Minty for almost 30 years or so. I knew your mother too, she was a part of the cause most of her life as well."

"Really? We don't know very much about her seeing as she died when we were eight or so."

"O yes, my dear your mother and her brother were the leading commanders during our time. Your mother being the strongest one, always volunteering for missions and rallying negroes on the plantations to fight for what they believe. She sparked so many revolts and takeovers that she began to be known as "Spama". She even helped a man by the name of Nat Turner start a revolt a long time ago, but it ended badly after he gained enough people to believe he was bigger than the entire picture."

" I remember people calling my mother "Spama" a long time ago. I just thought it was some type of nickname."

"It is, baby. It's ancient Blackfoot that means spark."

"Well, can you explain why Minty is so tough on us? We just met her not too long ago, and she treats us like we are cowards and don't know anything."

"Well, baby if I don't know anything about old Minty, I do know that she has been a force in this journey of our people since your mother passed. I have seen her every time she has went out and every time she came here, she asked about the state of the black man not being ready for battle. Eventually, her concern over time became a worry and then a resentment."

"I never thought about it like that."

"She knows, but she can't help but believe what she has seen happen time and time again even before you were born."

"And as far as treating us like we don't know anything?"

"Well, you don't. Before you got here, you didn't know you knew a language that was here before all of us. Just because you are educated, doesn't mean you know enough. Listen to Minty, because she will keep you alive, you hear me?"

"Yes ma'am," they both said to Ms. Darlene as they finished their breakfast. "Good, now you two go head and finish your food so that you can get some rest. We don't have a lot of time, and you two have a big night ahead of you."

"Why is that?"

"Because tonight I will be telling you what you need to know to stay alive and you need your energy so that you can remember."

"I think on that note I will go to sleep. Lord knows I want to stay alive."

"I am glad you agree, the children will take you to where you will be sleeping." The twins then get up from the table and follow one of the children outside as she walks toward the other house. She gets to the adjacent house, and instead of walking

279

into it she walks behind, where there is a large tree line. She stops in front of one of them and says, "Who wants to sleep closer to the ground?"

"What? I thought we were going to go into the house where there are beds."

"No, we don't sleep in those houses until it gets too cold to sleep outside."

"Why?"

"Because we don't want people to surprise us while we are sleeping."

The child then looks up into the trees and climbs it with ease. She reaches one of the branches and runs across it eventually jumping into the leaves. As the twins gasp and move into position to try to catch her, she falls and eventually lands into what seems to be a well-hidden hammock and lays there as the tree settles back into its untouched position.

She then stands up and jumps up and down in the hammock to give herself enough lift to jump back into the tree and climb down. She reaches the ground and says, "There you go, I will come and get you when Ms. Darlene is ready for you, later on tonight."

"How in the world are we supposed to get up there like you did? I mean I know how to climb a tree, but you just did something that I never saw before!"

"Remember at breakfast what Minty said?"

"What is that?"

"That just because you don't remember, doesn't mean you don't know. Just try." Mark looks up at the tree for a moment and runs completely up the trunk of it without using his hands. He gets to the branches and almost falls from being so surprised at what he had just done. He then runs across the branch and jumps into the hammock, just like the little girl had done moments before.

Matthew looks up in disbelief and then looks back at the little girl. She finally says, "What are you waiting for?"

Matthew does exactly what his brother had done before him and jumps into an adjacent hammock. The little girl looks up and smiles. She then walks away and says, "I will come and get you when Ms. Darlene is ready."

"How will you know when that is?"

Mark says from inside the hammock.

"Because it will be my bedtime, and you are sleeping in my bed."

Mark looks over into the hammock and notices a small teddy bear sitting at his feet. He picks it up, holds it and falls asleep.

Later on that evening, just after nightfall the little girl goes back to the trees to wake Matthew and Mark. They wake up and follow her to the smallest of the three houses in the village. It is a one-room house that is made of wood and has small coins glued all over.

It is well lit with candles which are located in the inside of the room. The little girl walks them to the store and says, "Ms. Darlene is in there. I know that I will probably never see you two again, so I just want to say good luck and I hope that you make it back."

Thank you, they both say as they walk into the house.

They look around and see Ms. Darlene sitting in the middle of the room with Minty sitting in the corner. In front of Ms. Darlene are three small circles. Each containing a different thing. The first circle has a small clay glass with water inside of it. The second circle had a candle which was burning, and the third circle has a small pile of dry leaves.

Ms. Darlene looks up at the two boys and says, "Welcome, I hope that you got enough rest. After this, you will have to go on your way, so pay attention and make sure you listen to everything that is said here tonight. Now please sit down so that we can begin."

The twins look over at Minty, and she signals for them to sit in front of Ms. Darlene. They both sit in front of her, and she smiles and says, "Thank you. Now is there anything you would like to ask or say before we start? Because after this is over, there is no more to be said for now."

Mark and Matthew look at each other and then Mark says, "I just want to say that sleeping in those trees was the best sleep I have ever gotten in my life. I am so serious, I slept like a baby."

"You are very welcome, so now can we begin?"

Ms. Darlene takes the candle from the circle and lights the pile of leaves on fire. As the leaves start to burn, Ms. Darlene starts to talk in a language that was different than what they had heard before. The leaves begin to change colors from blue to a dark orange and then back to blue again. Ms. Darlene takes the water in the clay cup and pours it on the leaves causing it to smoke. She says a couple of more things and the smoke begins to turn like a small tornado. The more she talks over the smoke, the stronger it starts to turn, creating lighting within itself. She leans over the top of the small tornado, looks inside of it and says to the men.

"It is important that you listen to everything that is said to you, because people with great words will try to trick you. There will be one person outside of this room that will help you along the way. That person will be who you least expect because you will not believe in him."

She pauses for a second looking down into the tornado in disbelief. She looks up at the twins and then looks back into the tornado and says, "One of you will not return, but just know that it will be for the greater good of our people. So accept your fate, and remember there is more to you than you can remember."

The tornado begins to slow down and then finally stops. Ms. Darlene gets up from where she was sitting and says to them.

"Now you must leave you have a lot of ground to make to catch up, they are in a small town 20 miles north from here called Habersham. Make sure you remember that song he left for you, it will point you right to him."

"How did you know about that song?"

"Ms. Darlene hears a lot about everything, child. Even when she doesn't want to."
" So that's all you're going to tell us?"

"Yes."

"You knew about the song, and that is all the information you can give us?"

"Ms. Darlene is like every other person in this world, child. She knows more about what has happened than what is to come. Now, it is time for you to go, remember what I said to you."

Ms. Darlene begins to clean the room as the boys walk out of the house in confusion. Minty stands up and before she can walk out Ms. Darlene hugs her and says, "You must listen to me. I know this will be hard for you, but you have to make sure that they stay together until the journey is complete. No matter what they do you must make sure that they see this thing through to the end together, do you hear me?"

"Yes, but is it that important?"

"Yes, because it is the only way I will ever see you again. Now give me a hug so you can make sure those babies stay safe. I have made some food for you to take with so you will have something out there."

"Thank you, Darlene. For everything."

"You can thank me by following my instructions."

Minty nods her head agreeing with Ms. Darlene as she walks out to retrieve the supplies and food Darlene has prepared for her to take with them.

As they are leaving, all of the children and Ms. Darlene are standing in the open area waiting for Minty and the twins to get to the edge of the forest. Minty contemplates what Ms. Darlene has said to her, knowing how she feels about Negroes that don't listen, but she knows that everything she has said thus far has made sense and ultimately saved her life. So, despite what her gut is telling her, she vows to listen to Ms. Darlene as she always has.

The twins both follow behind Minty and think about what Ms. Darlene has said to them. This is the first time they have ever experienced anything like this in their lives, so it is hard for them to grasp what is going on. Mark out of frustration looks over at his brother and quietly says, "All I wanted to do was go and find Nathan before they kill him. Now, we are in the middle of nowhere climbing trees like a monkey, speaking in a language we didn't know was a language at all. Oh, and don't forget reading our future in the eye of a small tornado. What do you think she means by trusting someone that we never would?"

"I don't know, but what I do know is Minty is still alive because of her, so I'm going to do whatever it is that she said. I just hope when we see it we recognize it."

"Would you two stop talking so much and come on! We already have a lot of ground to cover before the morning. Let's say goodbye and get going."

They reach the end of the forest line where Ms. Darlene stands with open arms to hug her dear friend. The twins wait next to the children while they have a small talk. The children look at them and smile until Minty calls them over to where they are.

Ms. Darlene hugs Minty again and says to her, "Remember what I said, darling. No matter what remember what I said to you. Make sure you're safe and can come back and see me, okay?"

"Okay."

They hug again, and then Ms. Darlene calls the twins over to talk to them. "Ms. Minty is a fine woman you two. Better than you will ever know. She has saved a lot of lives including my own, and I am forever grateful. Remember to listen to her and what I have told you so that you may return as well."

Yes ma'am, they both say as Ms. Darlene hugs them both before she sends them into the night. As they walk into the forest, one of the children stops them and says, "it was good meeting you and good luck. I hope you are successful and make it back."

"Thank you," the twins say to the little girl. She hugs them both then looks at them and says, "Remember, if you ever come here without Ms. Minty you should know her first name. I would hate to have to kill you because you don't."

The little girls smile at them and runs toward the trees. The twins see her run up the trunk of the tree and disappear into the branches and leaves. The tree shifts as if it was catching the little girls in its arms and calms to a slow breeze. "I have got to get one of those when we get home, seriously."

Minty and the twins eventually disappear into the forest as Ms. Darlene offers up one last prayer for her friend, then mumbles to herself, claps her hands softly in praise and turns back toward the village. She knows that Minty will follow her instructions, but is concerned that the twins will not do the same. As she walks back toward the village, she turns one more time to look at the space they all disappeared in and smiles.

Chapter 14

(November 1, 1897) - Late night - Mr. and Mrs. Lesure

Mr. and Mrs. Lesure sit in their library having a conversation. Mrs. Lesure is knitting in her chair while Mr. Lesure reads a book and has a late night drink.

Mr. Lesure getting aggravated by what he is reading in the local paper says to his wife.

"My father would be beside himself if he was still alive to see what this country is turning into."

"What do you mean by that?"

"Look at all of the revolts that have been going on around this country since William Mckinley took over as president. In May the city of Nashville had an explosion that illuminated the city with electric lights. The Mine Workers Union was formed and now people who work there only have to work eight hours a day and I hear they are trying to get wage increases. One of the greatest writers of our time Mark Twain was rumored to have died, and then three months later Mark Twain writes a letter in the New York Journal saying it isn't true. My good friend James Z. George dies leaving the Senate of Mississippi in question. And to top all of that off there is a French feminist newspaper in the works by the name of La Fronde."

Next thing you know, the niggers of this country will feel as if they are equal to us and want their own newspaper.

"Is that such a bad thing? I mean the woman that founded the newspaper is only expressing her concerns about trying to become a psychiatrist in a world where only men don't agree."

"Well, it is a scientific fact that a woman can not treat patients properly because of the way they are built mentally. With the problems you all have once a month and how emotional you

294

can be, how do you expect to help an able bodied man to figure out his own problems?"

Mr. Lesure says somewhat laughing at his wife's comments.

"So, Mr. Lesure so that I am sure I understand you right you are saying that the only humans that have the capacity to teach and direct the rest of the world are white males?"

"Well, since the beginning of time the white man has been in control. There is no reason why it should change now."

"You know I was reading somewhere that the African was the first ethnic group in the world. And that they had established a lot of things that we call state of the art today."

Mr. Lesure takes off his reading glasses and says to his wife.

"Is that so, Mrs. Lesure? Then tell me why the white male seems to be running this world. From Europe all the way to the new Americas the white man has been the force that makes the wheel turn. So, explain to me if the African was the first to do all of these things then why are they not in control?"

Mrs. Lesure never looks up from her knitting and thinks for a moment about Mr. Lesure's question.

Feeling as if he has stumped his wife, Mr. Lesure asks again.

"So Elizabeth, have you come up with an answer?"

"Well, I believe that the only thing the white man has done in success is making the rest of the world believe he is superior to them."

"What do you mean?"

"Well, the white male never invented ships, nor navigation yet we believe he did. We live in a country where most new inventions come from the people who need it to make jobs easier, yet they cannot go to the office of patents and make any money from it. I believe the white male has done well at taking something and making it his own, but to call him superior is a stretch."

Mr. Lesure looks over at his wife in disbelief. He says to her, "Well, Elizabeth I never thought I would hear you say something like that against white Americans."

"Well, what did I say wrong? I never put any other race above us by what I was saying. All I said was the truth."

"And what was that?"

"That the white males of today were smart by making people believe if it is on paper it means its legal. Even though to use paper and write is only for them."

As she finishes her sentence, a negro maid servant that came into the room to retrieve Mr. Lesure's glass drops a tray she brought into the room. She bends down to pick up the mess in shock of what Mrs. Lesure has said to her husband. Mr. Lesure sees it as his negro servant is being clumsy and says, "See, how can you expect someone that can't even hold a tray without dropping it to help make this country great?"

Mrs. Lesure looks up at her husband and says, "Well, I seem to recall when we met you weren't the most coordinated man I have ever met. Yet, here you are in the Senate in the great state of Georgia."

Mr. Lesure is a little upset at the conversation. As the two look at each other, Mr.
Lesure calms himself enough to say to his wife.

"On that note, I think I will retire for the night. Will you be joining me?"

"In a minute, dear. I want to work on this a little more before I come into the bedroom."

Mr. Lesure stands up and walks over to his wife kissing her on the forehead. She looks up at him and smiles, and he walks out of the room.

Moments later the maid servant that dropped the tray returns with a drink on the same tray. Mrs. Lesure looks at her and says, "Mr. Lesure has retired for the evening so he won't be needing another glass, thank you."

"I know that, Mrs. Lesure. I took the liberty of making you a drink seeing as to the conversation you had with the mister a little while ago."

Mrs. Lesure looks at the girl for a moment then takes the drink off of the tray. She sips it and says, "O, this is good! What is it?"

"A little whiskey and lemonade, my papi always said whiskey was too strong by itself, but if you add just a little lemonade to it, then you have a refreshing drink."

"Well, your papi was right! Thank you."

"No, Mrs. Lesure thank you. If more whites thought like you this country would be a beautiful place."

The maid servant walks out of the room, and Mrs. Lesure finishes her drink in silence while working on her knitting.

Following Minty - Mark, Matthew, and Minty

Minty and the twins had been walking for hours through the forest trying to make up time. Minty walks alone ahead of the boys thinking to herself what could possibly be the reason for Ms. Darlene's concern. The twins walk behind her talking about what is next in the journey and realize that things are more than they seem.

"Did you see how I ran up that tree? I mean I have done things like run up a wall or jump a fence quicker than other people but never thought anything about it. Now, all of a sudden I can run up a tree a hundred feet tall with ease. I mean, what else can we do?"

"I don't know, but what I do know is whatever is about to happen is going to change our lives forever. I just hope in the end it's for something good."

Matthew stares at Minty from a distance watching her as she walks in front of her in the moonlight. She walks as if she knows the area and is confident in their direction. The moon is bright, and because the night is cool, there are no dangers in site. As Matthew watches Minty in front of him, he is reminded of his own mother and how she carried herself. So many things have been revealed to him and his brother, that they can't help but wonder.

Mark looks to the east and sees a small home with a light coming out of a window upstairs. He thinks about his father for a moment and wonders what things were like before they were born. He turns and says to his brother, "Do you ever think about mom sometimes?"

"Yea, I think about her a lot, and I wonder what things would have been like if she didn't die when we were kids."

"Yea, and from what we learned I wonder what other things we could have been doing other than growing up in Marthasville. I always wondered why I was so hostile to white folks like they wouldn't string me up at any given moment."

They both walk for a while in silence following Minty until Matthew says, "I'm going to go and talk to her."

"About what?"

"Things that we don't know."

Matthew walks ahead of his brother catching up to Minty to talk for a moment. Minty hears him coming and looks back for a moment in disbelief, she continues to walk when Matthew catches up to her and says, "Hi."

"Hello, this is a first."

"What do you mean?"

"Well, I have been doing this for more than 30 years, and I can't say that I have ever had a man walk with me during a journey."

"Why is that?"

"Well, because he either is too scared but doesn't want to turn away, or he wants to control the journey because he doesn't feel that I can."

"Well, that's not why I came to talk to you."

"Okay, well about what?"

"I think I would like to know why things are the way they are. I mean, the war has been over for 30 years now, and things still seem to be the same way they were before it happened?"

Minty looks over at Matthew in shock at his questions. Never before has a man talked to her as if he didn't have the answers already. Minty looks at Matthew for a moment and almost smiles at the hope of her people before saying, "Well, I guess the first thing I should ask you is what do you know about the Civil War?"

"Well, I know that Lincoln wanted to free the slaves because he felt that we were human beings just like anyone else. But I guess in the end it was to make sure that the same ideas were shared all over the country, just not the south."

"Wrong."

"Well, what do you mean?"

"Well, the civil war was not about freeing slaves at all. After so many takeovers all over the country, they had to decide if they were going to be one country united against the black man or take the risk of us doing what they have always feared."

"And what is that?"

"Black people figuring out that they were no longer the minority." "What do you mean by that?"

"The Civil War should have never been the north vs the south, at all. It should have been the American Negro against his oppressor in the white man. But, instead, we befriended them, even taking the side of the white man knowing that what they were doing was wrong. And that continued how they treated us to this day."

"I never really thought about it like that."

"Well, let's start off from the beginning. In the history of the world, every other race has its own God. But we are the only race of people that are taught to pray to a God that doesn't look like them. Which tells them without saying it out loud that you they will never be in the image of him, and that they should obey anyone that looks like the pictures that hang in our house. Now tell me, Matthew, what does Jesus look like?"

"White."

"Yet, the bible tells you that his skin was like bronze and hair like wool, but yet when shown a picture, Jesus looks nothing like that. Have you ever wondered why that is?"

"Yes, I have."

"Then you are just as much the problem."

"Why would you say that?"

"Because you never took the time to find out anything different, you just did what you were told to do. That has been the problem with us since we got to this beautiful country. It's time for us to be just as proud of ourselves as they are to their own or we will always be a second class citizen, no matter what they try to make us believe."

Minty walks off into the moonlight as Matthew gets caught in some small branches. Mark catches up to his brother and helps him untangle himself and says to Matthew, "She just gone leave you here and didn't even help you?"

"Yes, but I think it's because she wants me to start helping myself."

The twins continue to walk behind Minty into the moonlight so that they can reach their friend in time.

Matthew starts to think more about the state of his people in America and less about believing in the system. For years Matthew has always thought that the system set in place was going to eventually help him and his family become a first class citizen. But the comments that Minty had just told him makes him question the very idea of what he has been reading and told over the years.

"Will I ever truly be a part of this country or will I only be allowed to be the machine that makes it work?" he asks himself as they continue to walk toward Habersham.

Chapter 15

Nathan and Robert - (November 24, 1897) - Talking it through/Music and Money

Nathan has been a prisoner of Robert's for a month, everyone sees Nathan chained to the back of Robert's carriage but thinks nothing of it because it is common. Nathan is exhausted by the time they reach Habersham from not eating and only getting rest when Nathan and his band mates decided to stop for the night. When they did stop to eat and drink they would pass the time by throwing rocks at Nathan calling him "nigger" and any other name that they could come up with.

They finally stop right outside of a town called Habersham because they have run out of food and money to buy it with. Robert has to come up with a way to make money quickly, so he goes to talk to a local bar owner to see if he and his band can play for food and rooms.

So the next day they walk into town with Nathan to ask the bar owner about working for him. It's a growing town with hotels, a grocery, and bank. Nathan walks by a boutique that has a dress and a man's suit in the window. The dress makes him think about Mrs. Debbie because it is made for a bigger woman. He smiles to himself thinking about her. But just as he begins to daydream about better times, one of Robert's band members punches him in the stomach and says, "Mind your manners, nigger. This isn't the kind of town niggers are allowed to smile in, in public. If you feel you need to smile or anything like that you go over to that bucket and stick your face in it."

The man points to a bucket on each side of every building. Just then there is a Negro man talking to another. The Negro picks up the bucket during the quick conversation and puts his head inside the bucket so that he can laugh at what was said. Nathan is shocked to see this, and it shows on his face. The man smiles and says to him, "See how good you had it? The niggers over here know their place, and you will to in just a little while."

Robert and his band walk up to a bar that seems to be closed at the time. The building is two stories with a saloon door that is open as the owner is sweeping the floor. Outside of the saloon is a small piano resting along the building. The saloon owner sweeps the dirt outside of the saloon and notices Robert and the group of men he was with and asked, "The bar doesn't open for an hour or so. Can I help you fellas with anything else?"
"Yes, Sir. We are a traveling band looking for work, and we were wondering if we could possibly audition for you?"

The man looks at Robert and then at Nathan and says to him, "Is the nigger in the band? Because if he is, I will have to say no. We don't allow niggers in this here bar."

"No, Sir. He is just with us because we saw him wondering when we were traveling this way. Figure we can take him over to the sheriff here in town to send him to one of those new big jails they are building across the country."

"That would be best, shouldn't have a nigger just wondering like a free man around these parts. Come on in, but you will have to leave the nigger outside."

"Yes, sir."

The saloon owner looks over at Nathan and spits in his direction, then walks into the saloon waiting on Robert and his band members to enter the building.

Robert takes the chains that are being used to shackle Nathan and wraps the opposite end to a post most people tie their horses to when visiting the area. Robert's band mates go into the saloon as Robert stays behind to talk to Nathan.

"Now boy you're in a very bad situation here. See, the people of this town don't like niggers around. So, try not to draw any attention to yourself or you will be dead before we can get you out of here, do you understand?"

"Yes."

"Good, I'll be back shortly to get you. Hopefully, the children that walk past don't throw stones at you that could break something. Because if the jails can't use you, then we will just have to put you down like a sick horse."

Robert smacks Nathan on the back and walks into the saloon to talk to the owner. Nathan looks around and notices a group of children watching him, laughing and looking for rocks to throw. Nathan looks over at the piano sitting along the building and sits in the chair next to it.

Inside the saloon, Robert and his band perform for the owner and from the start, the owner is not pleased. Nathan listens in to their audition and shakes his head at what he is hearing. At that same moment, the children that were once laughing at Nathan are now throwing small rocks at him and inviting their friends to do the same. A lady says to her friend while watching this all happen, "It's just like that nigger game at the carnivals. Right here in our very own town. What a fun thing for the kids."

As the crowd of people gets bigger as they are noticing Nathan in their town. Nathan has to try to find shelter of some sort to protect himself from what he knows will happen. He tries to walk away but is reminded by the chains that hold I'm to the building. He walks to one side of the building and can see a small group of white men walking in his direction. He goes to the other side of the building and sees the children in the alley trying to find bigger rocks to throw. He walks back to where he was when it all began and saw the piano, he sits in front of it and begins to play.
At the same time, Robert and his band are finishing up their performance. The owner of the saloon is not happy at what he has just heard and says to Robert and his companions.

"I just don't think there is any room here for the sound you gentlemen have. Honestly, you sound like you can play the instruments, just not together. I'm sorry fellas, but I have a big business here, and I need a band that will bring in the

314

customers and keep them here. I just bought a new piano, so I have to make sure I can pay for it with the person sitting behind it."

Just as the men are leaving the saloon, they overhear what Nathan is playing outside on the old piano sitting along the building. They can hear Nathan singing.

"The days we spend

The times we share

All alone at this piano

Wishing you were there

But through it all I sing out loud

Knowing that you are listening

And hope that you are proud."

The men step outside of the saloon and see most of the town listening to Nathan play the piano. Robert begins to get upset at the fact that Nathan has caused such a crowd to gather, but before he can do anything about Nathan's singing, the saloon owner says, "Now that is the sound that will get the people-in-here! If he wasn't a nigger, you would have yourself a deal!"

Robert thinks for a moment about what the saloon owner has said to him and then says, "Well, he is with us. He is a songwriter. We were just showing you that we could play the instruments, but he is the one that writes all of the songs. That's why we brought him into town so that you could see him as well."

"But we don't allow niggers in our saloon."

"I know, we just brought him with us so that you can see what type of music we will be playing."

The saloon owner looks at Robert for a moment and thinks it through. He spits some tobacco out onto the street and says to Robert, "The cash payment is based on how we do for the week. We will give you room and board in the hotel across the street as well as meals. But the nigger can not stay, of course you know that. The more people you bring in, the better the pay is at the end of the week is that a deal?"

"You have a deal. We will lock up our nigger outside of town, but we would love to stay in your hotel. You have a deal."

They both continue to listen to Nathan play the piano until the local sheriff had seen enough and dismissed the crowd of people to go on their way.

(November 24, 1897) - Minty, Matthew, and Mark

"Not paying attention will get you killed."

Minty and the twins have been walking through the forest all night trying to catch up to Nathan. As the night turned into the daytime, Minty at first light starts to look for a safe place to stay out of sight until nightfall. As she starts to slow down her pace looking for a place to rest, Mark continues on walking so that he can make up the time spent with Ms. Darlene.

Minty says nothing as Mark continues to walk past her as if she knows or has seen this before. She shakes her head and continues on preparing a spot on the ground for her to lay down on. Matthew sees his brother continuing on through the forest and looks over at Minty to see if she will say anything. As Mark gets further away, Matthew turns to Minty and says, "Are you going to say anything to him?"

"No."

"Why not?"

"Because there is no point, once a black man has made up his mind there is no turning back. All you can do is hope he will be safe."

"Well, I will at least try."

"I think it is too late for that, Matthew. His choice has gotten him into a little trouble."

Minty looks over Matthew's shoulder in the woods to see Mark being arrested by three white men and taken away. Matthew knows that if he tries to rescue his brother, they both will be in jail. Matthew watches his brother as they take him away, he then turns around and finds Minty asleep on the ground with her hat in her face to keep the sun off. Matthew looks in disbelief, walks over to Minty and says quietly, "So are we going to just let him be taken away to some jail in the nearest town?" "No, he chose to keep going when he saw me stop to rest. So we are not going to let him do anything because he did it himself. Besides, he won't be going to no jail in town when we are only three miles from a penitentiary anyway."

"Penitentiary? Are you talking about those new building they have been building putting all the negroes they can find in?"

319

"Yes, Sir. They built the one not too far from here about 30 years ago. Don't worry because they only build roads and train rails for the railroads. None of that back breaking work the other prisons are doing, cause your brother wouldn't last a week."

"So are we just going to leave him in there?"

"I don't see any reason we should go get him out. So, unless you can think of a reason why we should risk our lives for someone who didn't think much of his own we will be right here for the next three days until things clear up."

"Clear up? What are you talking about? And why do we have to stay here for the next three days?"

"Well, seeing as this is Tuesday and your brother just got taken away means that the locals are on patrol for random Negroes with no business wandering around. Do you know how much they get for finding niggers? Makes me want to do it myself. Hell, I know some niggers that deserve it. Anyway, they make a camp and hang around for about three days and catch as many men as they can. So, we should stay here off the road until they are gone."

"Are you telling me that just because we are walking through the forest, they can take us away?"

"No. I am telling you that if you don't have a pass from the plantation owner that says you can travel without him, you might end up in jail for the rest of your life. You have never been out of Marthasville have you?"

"No, this is our first time."

"Should have known. You better get some rest and get comfortable because we are going to be here for a while." Minty lays down in the spot that she has made for herself and goes to sleep.

Matthew sits up and thinks about how he is going to convince Minty to help her brother.

(November 25, 1897) - Mark meets the future

Mark walks out of the tree line into the road where there are three white men sitting around a small fire drinking coffee and talking. Mark walks out of the forest and is immediately seen by the men who yell at him and say, "Hey, Nigger! Come over here right now!"

"Who are you talking too?!"

"I think you are the only nigger that we can see out here unless there are more with you!"

Mark looks around to see if Minty and his brother happen to have been following him. He sees that they were still inside the forest where they could be seen, so he moves away from the opening he has just walked out of so that the men will not look back for his path. As the men continue to get closer, Mark remembers his training with Emmet about sometimes having to play meek, and as much as he doesn't want to, he knows that it could cost him his life and even his brothers.

"Nigger, what are you doing out here by yourself? There isn't a plantation for miles from here, don't tell us you are one of those "I'm free" niggers, are you?"

"I am free, sir. I was walking this way to visit my aunt over in Habersham not too far from here."

"Well, do you have a permission pass from your plantation owner?" "No. I told you I was a free man."

"Yes, but how do we know you have a job at all? We can't just have niggers walking around here going where ever they want. We just gave you the right to be paid for working, not to go and come as you please."

"You better come with us, boy. Before you get caught by someone that would love to have a hanging."

"Where are you taking me?"

"Well, seeing is that you don't have a pass and we don't know exactly where you are coming from, we have to take you over to the jail."

Mark thinks to himself how easy it would be to get rid of the men but knows that his brother would not leave him in jail. He looks back one last time at the opening to the forest where he had walked out of and says a small prayer to himself before they take him away.

"Dear, God please give Minty and Matthew the strength to come and find me." Before Mark could spell his name out loud, he was booked into jail and sent through processing. Mark is standing in line to take his photo for the prison records, and as he walks up to the camera, the officer says to his supervisor, "Sir, the camera has seemed to stop working."

"Damn it! That is the second time in three weeks that has happened. Where have we been sending it to be repaired?"

"Sears Roebuck & Co. This is the second camera we have received in two weeks, and we are having the same problems."

"Well, send them another telegraph and get these prisoners outside before rec is over. Then bring them back in and assign them cells."

"Yes, sir!"

As the supervisor leaves the room, the officer says to the inmates inside of the room, "Okay, inmates! Everyone outside in the yard! And when you come back, I will make sure you have a comfy bed to share with the rats for the night!"

The men were all led outside into an open area where all of the inmates were for daily exercise. As Mark walked out of the dirty building, he sees an open field that is surrounded by the forest he was arrested outside of. There is a small baseball field in the far left end of the field surrounded by a track. On the other side of the yard is nothing but groups of people standing around talking. The whites with the whites, Indians with the Indians, and the blacks with the blacks. But as Mark looks a little closer, he notices a black man sitting by himself in the far end of the yard.

Mark walks passed all of the groups despite being watched by them all. He passes the whites who give him a mean glare for being the new nigger on the yard. One yells out as he passes, "One more nigger we are going to have to get in-line or kill."

Mark pays no attention to the white man. This is something that he has heard before. So it doesn't bother him as he walks passed the Indian men when one says to another, "He seems to be a half breed, he is not a full Indian man so let him live with the niggers, they will accept him."

Mark hears the conversation and is somewhat bothered by it, but not enough to stop walking toward the black man at the end of the yard. He continues to walk as one of the black men turn to greet him. He is a tall, muscular man with no shirt, a pair of pants, and no shoes. Mark has seen a man like this before in his own life and decides to stay as far away from him as possible. But as Mark passes him to still walk in the direction of the old man he is grabbed by the arm.

Mark turns in the direction of the man holding his arm as the muscular man starts to speak to him, "I was talking to you. My name is Paul, but people around here call me Tiny. If you have any questions or need anything around here, you just let me know."

"I have one question for you."

"See, I knew you would see it my way. What's that?"

"Does your little dog know how easy it is to get your arm broken in half?"

"I don't think so."

Mark grabs the man by the hand and bends his arm backward forcing him to the ground on one knee. Mark continues to talk to Tiny and say, "Well, tell him that it is easier than one person may think. And the next time he even thinks about touching me or anyone else for that matter, to remember how this felt."

Mark lets the man go and continues to walk over to the old man who is now watching all of this happen. As Mark approaches the man he looks down at his papers, which Mark can now see are drawings and says to him as he reaches him, "I don't have anything to give you but these pictures. I don't want any trouble, and I am too old to fight so take what you want and just leave me alone."

"I don't want anything from you, sir. I just noticed and realized that you are probably the only person on this field that seems to stay out of trouble. And I figured if there was anyone here that could show me the way on how to stay out of trouble, it would be you."

The man looks up at Mark to see his face, then looks back down at his drawing and says to him, "Well, if you are going to stay out of trouble, what you need to do is find a way to stay away from that man that tried to talk to you."

"You mean Tiny and his helper?"

"Yes, and seeing what you did and the fact I am talking to you, I figure I should tell you my name. The name is Albert, son."
"Hello, Albert. My name is Mark, and I hope I am not getting you in any trouble by talking to you."

"Me in any trouble, no. I have been here since they opened this place. So everybody, including the guards leave me alone. But, you might be in a little trouble, seeing as I haven't spoken to anyone else but the guards and now you, since I have been here."

Just as he finishes his sentence to Mark, Tiny walks over to them both. He knocks the papers out of Albert's hands and onto the ground and says to Mark, "I know that this is your first day here and you must be confused about what is going on, so I will give you another chance. My name is Tiny, and I run this place, anything you need or want you just ask me, and I will see what I can do. But, if you choose to not take my help and hurt my fellow inmates I can't help you."

"Well, as much as I thank you for showing me the way, I think I will stick to myself and Albert if you don't mind."

Mark bends down to help Albert pick up his drawings. Tiny walks over and steps on a piece of paper that Mark is trying to pick up and says, "If you keep up with how you are acting, paper won't be the only thing you are on your knees for."

Mark sweeps Tiny's legs, and he falls on his back. Mark puts his knee in Tiny's chest and says to him, "Well, that means if I am on my knees I will have to make sure you are under them."

Before Tiny and his group of friends can get to Matthew and his new friend Albert, the prison officer, comes out and says, "Time for all of you to come in! For those of you that haven't found someone to share a cell with already you will be assigned to one shortly."

Albert looks over at Mark and says to him, "Seeing that if you let them pick for you, you will end up in a cell with one of Tiny's workers. I have never had a cellmate in the 30 years I have been here. I think you should bunk with me."

"Thank you, Albert. It would be an honor."

Mark and Albert walk pass Tiny and his men, and exchange looks. Mark walks backward into the prison so that he can keep an eye on the men and then disappears into the dark hallway. As he turns toward Albert and follows him to his cell, he can hear Tiny outside say to his men, "He is going to be here for a while. We got plenty of time to make him understand the rules."

Chapter 16

(November 26, 1897) - Minty's Concerns

Minty wakes up late in the night to find Matthew sitting at attention watching their surroundings. Minty sits up and lays against the tree she was under and looks at Matthew waiting for him to start to tell her why they should retrieve his brother.

Matthew knows that it is very important to ask the right questions so that her brother can be freed, so instead of telling Minty why she should free him, he starts off with a question, "Why don't you like my brother?"

"It's not that I don't like him. There are just certain things he does that I don't like."

"If you don't mind me asking what are those things?"

Minty now sits up straight against the tree and starts to speak.

"Well, that's the first time anyone has asked me a question like that, so let me think about it."

Minty takes out some of the things that they had packed for the journey and starts to make a small meal for the both of them.

"I think if I had to start with something it would be the stubbornness of the black man in America. I mean I have never seen any other man be enslaved for such a long time and then once they are freed, act like they deserve to be respected."

"What do you mean?"

"Slavery went on in America for 300 years. Never once did the black man as a whole ask for respect from the white man until the white man told him he was free. Sure, there were people like Charles Deslondes out of Louisiana or Nat Turner from Virginia, but they were left by themselves when it came to true

334

support. Most of the times when black people did come together there was always one negro that undermined the cause or quit when things got hard for them. And for that, we will always be second class to any other race because we don't even know how to take care of ourselves. Any more questions?"

"No."

"Why not?"

"Well, because I have to make sure what I say is enough to make you think different. I don't want to be stubborn and think that I know all the questions."

Matthew lays down and goes to sleep as Minty thinks about what he has just said.

Mark and Albert are laying in their beds after being locked in the cell for the night. Mark looks around the cell at different drawings Albert has done over the years he has been in jail. On one of the early paintings is a negro man standing next to an Indian chief watching a village from a distance, burn to the ground.

Mark moves around the room and notices another painting of the same two men watching the same village, but in this picture, the men notice that the people of the burned village are rebuilding and putting things back together. But behind them in the distance, there are two small fires starting in the villages they come from.

Mark moves around the room again and sees another picture with the same two men running away to their villages after the fire has spread wild, while the village they originally watched burn down looks better than it did before, with taller buildings and houses.

Mark finally moves around the room to see the final picture of the Negro and Indian man complaining to the man who is white from the original burning village. He stands and smiles as the two men argue with him while both of their villages burned to the ground.

Mark looks over at Albert and says to him, "What do these pictures mean, Albert?"

"You know I have been here for 30 years, and no one has ever asked that question."

"I think they are great pictures. But I wonder what you are trying to say."

"Well, the first painting is the self-destruction of the white race. See, a long time ago whites were no better than any other race. The difference was they saw it happening and tried to fix it while it was happening."

The second picture is the Indian and the Negro finally realizing that their villages were on fire too, but by the time they realized what was going on, the villages were almost burned to the ground. While the white man's village was rebuilt better than before with the help of the community.

And the last picture is of the Indian and the Negro complaining to the White man about his village burning down, but see they never took the time to put the fire out and rebuild.

They just complained to the person they thought was their problem. "Well, aren't the white people in this country the reason we are in the state we are in now?"

"Depends on who you ask. Most people will say that the whites are the root of evil, and maybe they are right, but one thing that is a fact is that the Indian and the Negro were the original man."

"So?"

"So, I will ask you this. If the Indian and the Negro were the original man then why are we following the white laws and government?"

"I don't know."

"It's because we as a people were more concerned about watching their fires and problems than our own villages, and when we finally realized what was happening it was almost too late to fix, but instead of going back to our own villages to rebuild and make them stronger. We blamed the white man for our problems thus putting him in charge."

"I see that, but how did we put the white man in charge? Isn't he the reason things are the way they are?"

"No. Things are the way they are because we didn't rebuild. And the reason he is in charge is because we gave him that position when we gave them control of our problems. And then waited on them to fix them."
"I never thought of it like that."

"Most people don't until they get too old to do anything about it. Now go to sleep, young man. We got a lot going on tomorrow."

"What's tomorrow?"

"We are working on the new roads in and out of town. So one day there will be machines that will take us everywhere instead of horses."

"Really? Are you talking about those new coal-driven machines?"

"The very same. So one day it will be the only way to get around on land."

"I don't know if I am ready for all of that."

"And that is exactly why we as a People will never move ahead of the world. Because we are too scared of advancing. Goodnight, young fella."

Albert blows out the single candle in the cell, as the reflection of the moon off of the floor lines the walls where they are sleeping. Mark stays up and thinks about what Albert has just taught him. Was he right about the Negro? Did we forget about our own problems so much so that we started to blame a race that shouldn't care anyway? He lays there most of the night thinking to himself until he falls asleep.

That same night, Matthew and Minty are quietly placing small rabbit traps around the forest for food. They only speak when Matthew is not sure of something, which strikes Minty as different.

Finally, after all the work they have done over the last couple of hours, they sit down to eat some of the food they had packed for the trip. Sitting in silence for most of their meal, Matthew finally says to Minty, "Why do you think that the Negro man is considered last in the world we live in? I mean for years we have been enslaved and treated a certain way. Why is it so easy for other races to treat us the way they do? I have heard stories about the Negro from Africa and how he is such a king. If that is the case then how did we get here? How did we allow the white man to bring us here to be sold and bought like a cow or deer?"

Minty looked at Matthew for a moment and then looked down at her food. Once again she has never been asked such a question, so she takes some time to actually think about her answer to Matthew.

"There was a time where slave trade was common in the Negro and white communities. It wasn't done to be an evil thing at the time, it created extra income and one less thing to worry about, by selling the strong men off to foreign lands. See, the original slaves were warriors from different tribes all over the country. And just like the tribes that were captured by their enemy they either became dead or slaves."

"So why was slavery so different than all those other places you talk about?"

"If I had to guess it would be because we were the only ones that sold our own to other people. Truth is we are children of outcasts, just like everyone else here in this country. But we didn't get the choice or chance to want to come here. This is a land of liberty for those who were told of a place of risk, hard work and wealth. Not for those who were brought here for labor, abuse and misleading. We were brought here for a different purpose, and that alone is a hard thing to get over. You know I even heard that America wasn't the only country that enslaved blacks. I heard most countries enslaved blacks over the last two hundred and something years. Just the other country outlawed if before America did."

"Do you think that is true? I mean that other countries had slaves too?"

"Yes, it happened, and it was our own fault."

"What do you mean?"

"You will learn, Matthew. In due time, young man you have a lot of life left." Minty watches Matthew as they sit in silence for the rest of the night wondering about what he is thinking. For the first time, she has encountered a man that has gained her interest. Matthew gives her hope in the black man but understands that he still hasn't given her a reason to free his brother. Deep down she hopes that he does because she knows in order to stay alive it must happen.

Chapter 17

(November 27, 1897) - Mark and Albert - The Chain Gang

Albert stands up and looks out of the bars of the cell before he wakes Mark up for the day. Albert did this every day in his cell, and for the first time, he realizes he is sharing a cell. He watches Mark sleep for a moment before he wakes him up, but before he says anything Mark wakes up himself.

"Good morning, Mr. Albert. What do they have in store for us today?"

"It's the chain gang for us, young man."

"Yea, I heard they were building railroads all down this way. After they burned down the city of Atlanta during the war, most of the stuff had to be rebuilt for us to function again. I guess freeing the slaves wasn't the only problems the south had."

"Freeing the slaves? When did that happen?"

"I forget you have been-in-here for years. About 30 years ago they finally made it a rule in this country that no one can be enslaved."

"Well, if that is the case then what do you think this here we are in is?"

"What do you mean, Albert?"

Just as Mark asks Albert a question, the man Mark now knows' as Tiny walks past them pushing Albert back into their cell. Tiny laughs as his goons surround Mark, he looks at Albert one more time and then says to Mark, "Look, I see that we got off on the wrong foot yesterday, so I want to start over. And seeing the way you handled one of my top guys in here I don't see any reason to try to bully you, so."

"So, what is it that you want from me?"

"Nothing, we just want you to know that we got your back in here and only want you to do the same when something happens around here. It's us against them, and if we have you we know, we can run this prison, including the guards."

"Is that so?"

"Yes, so all we need to know is if you are down with us or not?"

Mark looks around at the men standing in front of him and then at Albert standing inside the cell. Mark looks over at part of one of Albert's drawings that he can see from outside of the cell and then says to Tiny, "Well, it seems to me that if I join you, then you would be running this prison and not me. One, I don't fight for anything I don't believe in and two, there is nothing in this building worth believing in except my friend you just pushed into that cell there. So, what I need to happen is that you and your friends just move on and leave us alone before I show you all how angry I really can be."

One of Tiny's men walks toward Mark to confront him. Tiny seeing where this is going stops his friend and tries to change the subject so as nothing happens.

"I understand, you're new here, and you don't know us so why would you be on our side. Well, one day you're going to have to choose because this jail gives you no other choice. Or you will become just like your cell mate here." So are you two ready for the holiday coming up?

Mark looks over at Albert confused to what Tiny is talking about.

"I see, he hasn't told you yet. Well, tonight is the night the old lady comes to visit us. She does it every year, and the funny thing is she only visits your friend here. Word is she is a ghost that comes to us as a chicken at first, then she turns into a woman and talks to Albert here before disappearing again. That's why no one messes with him, hell even the guards are scared. A couple of years back there was one guard that actually saw the lady, and after he recovered from all his

348

injuries he quit, and I hear he has never been the same. Hope it don't happen to you too."

"Well, if it does it will be better then being here. Come on, Albert we gotta get to work before the guards come looking for us."

Mark walks over to Tiny, and he moves out of the way of the cell so that Albert is able to leave. He continues to watch Tiny and his group of friends until they are far enough away. Tiny continues to smile at Mark because he knows all he needs is time to convince Mark of what is law.
Mark and Albert continue out of prison and onto a truck that takes them to where to other inmates are working on an unfinished railway. Some men are ahead digging and moving wood into place while the men in front of Mark are putting the nails in place to make sure the railway stays.

Albert gets to the area where all the inmates from the jail are working and immediately gets to work. Mark not being told what to do, follows Albert's lead and helps him with the digging he has begun. Mark wants to ask so many questions to his new friend but doesn't know how. Why was being in prison considered being a slave to him?

And who was the chicken lady Tiny was talking about?

Their day continues on like this until late afternoon until they were given a small break for water and lunch. Mark and Albert receive their lunches and sit off to themselves to eat. Mark watches Albert for a moment and then asks him.

"So what did you mean about still being enslaved in here?"

Albert looks at Mark for a moment while he is still eating and laughs to himself.

He takes another bite of his food and says to Mark.

"Since the end of slavery, to be a black man in prison has become easier by the year. And more and more rules have been put into place for people like you and I to be here. And what is worse is that it's a teaching ground for men who aren't bad people to become bad."

"What do you mean?"

Albert pauses for a moment and then says to Mark. "You know that man we were talking to earlier before we left the prison?"

"Yea, Tiny what about him?"

"Well, when he first got here he wasn't Tiny his name was Jeremiah. He was a skinny kid twenty years ago, scared of his own shadow. He was put in here because he and his friends were hanging out together in front of a local store where he lived. He and his friends would sing in front of this store for hours, and the store owner would let them because it brought in customers."

That is until one day the local sheriff had enough and arrested the four boys under the Vagrancy Law, which allows any local authority to put you into the system for the smallest of reasons like hanging out in front of a store.

Well, when he got here he was scared and by himself. He cried for days to go home no matter what any of the other inmates would say to him. When he finally got a grip on what his life was going to be like he tried to make the best of things by being nice and helpful to the people he was locked in here with.

"Then what happened? Why is he so mean now?"

"Well, one day one of the guards started to take more of a liking to him than he should have. And no one here in the jail was brave enough to say anything about it, seeing that the guard became the warden less than 10 days later."

He would take Jeremiah to his office and we would hear him scream for hours but there was nothing we could do, that is until Jeremiah did it himself.

One day, when being escorted to the Warden's office, Jeremiah got a hold of a small blade about two inches long. The warden tried to molest Jeremiah as he always had, but this time

Jeremiah stuck that small knife into his neck. No one knew until one of the guards came to check and found the warden lying on the floor dead and Jeremiah sitting in his office chair playing with a toy train the warden kept on his desk.

"How is he still alive?"

"Well, because the prison didn't want to expose why he killed the warden, so they kept it under secrecy. And because none of the inmates liked the warden, having been put under some of the same situations before Jeremiah got here, they took Jeremiah in and showed him the way to make a way in here. They even gave him a nickname, in honor of the small knife he took with him that day to take care of the warden."

"Tiny."

"That's it. And ever since then he has just learned to become a better criminal, learning all the ways to manipulate and take advantage of any new inmate that enters this prison. Either you become part of his group to make it or become part of one of the other groups to make sure you stay alive against him. The only two people to have entered this jail and survive without his help are me and you."

"Does that bother you?"

"No, I have learned to walk this path alone to save my soul for a later day. The only thing I worry about is that you aren't as strong as you seem to be and one day you too will become more of a criminal than you are."

Off in the distance, Albert and Mark hear the guard yell, "Okay, men break time is over. Time to get back to the line and get to work!"

Mark gets up and follows Albert back to where they were working and begins to dig. Mark sees Albert struggling with a rock that needs to be moved and goes over to help him. They move the rock together, and Mark finally asks Albert, "So what about the old lady?"

"Son, if I told you about her I don't think you would understand."

"Well, I helped you with that heavy rock, and seems like we will be here for a while so try me."

"Son, a long time ago I had a life and today that life still haunts me. Just know that I am here because I want to be here, not because I have to be."

Matthew wakes up that evening with worry because he knows Minty is preparing to continue on without retrieving Mark from the jail. Before he opens his eyes, he can hear her gathering all of her things and prays one last time for his brother before he sits up. He wipes his eyes to see Minty starting a small fire to prepare something to eat before they leave.

"Good morning, Matthew. Would you like some coffee before we head on out? We have to get back to Marthasville so that I can get back to my own life."

"Yes, I would like some coffee. But, we are not going back to Marthasville."

"How so? We have been sitting here for three days now, the whites have gone back into their homes because they have gotten enough niggers out of this forest to pay for the rest of the winter's needs. And you have yet to tell me why I should help you get your brother out of jail. By now, I would have thought you would have come up with something, but instead, all you have done is watch me for the last couple of days."

"That is because I don't understand why."

"Why your brother is hardheaded? Well, I will tell you why. Since I can remember, all the men I have seen, other than my own father never listen to their woman. They instead blame us for the downfall of the nigger, saying that if we weren't so fearful, maybe we would be in a better place in this country. What they should be saying is why is it that the nigger man thinks he is here by himself? Why when you do have a strong nigger woman next to you, instead of being ashamed of her

356

standing tall and being fearless, you make it a point to discredit her mind and make her feel less of a person just because the world wants you to. That's what the white man does to his woman, but the difference is the white man is in control of this here country. And in the end, he decides what happens because he made the rules."

I heard once that in other countries they have queens running everything. That the strongest man kneels to her and follows her every command. Hell I even heard that even in Africa there use to be strong women helping run empires that lasted thousands of years. Do you think it's an accident now here in America that a woman is only good for bearing children and cocking their legs open?

"No, I don't. I think it was all set up that way so that we can never be whole as a People."

"Then you see why I will not go and rescue your brother."

Minty packs up the rest of her stuff and starts to walk away from Matthew

"So that's it,huh? You're just going to leave my brother in jail for something that he shouldn't be in there for?"

"That's my plan."

"So, what does that say about you?"

Minty stops in her path and turns to talk to Matthew, "And what is that suppose to mean?"

Matthew is nervous in giving his answer, but the love for his brother pushes through.

"I understand that you are mad at how we as men have treated our women over the years. We never came to your rescue when you needed us, letting the white man take-advantage of you behind closed doors. Sometimes in front of us and never raising a finger. I am ashamed of the fact that no matter what they did to us, we just took it and never fought back. But what about our women?"

"What about it?"

Matthew nervously clears his throat.

"Well, the one thing that I do see from white women is that no matter right or wrong she supports her man. Hell, have you ever met the O'Connor family up on the hill in Marthasville?"

"No, can't say that I have."

"Well, Mrs. O'Connor was one of the nicest people. She would give us fresh bread every time she made it to take home to our families to eat. Sometimes, she would even give us smoked meat her husband would bring back from hunting, just because."

"Well, her husband was gone a lot due to his job. He would tell us as kids that he was a traveling salesman, but we knew better because he didn't dress like the ones we had seen around town. Well, not too long ago a bounty hunter from Kansas came into town and claimed that Mr. O'Connor was a horse thief and was wanted in seven other states. Well, that man went over to the O'Connor house on the hill looking for Mr. O'Connor and found his wife sitting on the front porch making a scarf for her husband when he returned. That man took Mrs. O'Connor in the house and beat her 'til she was almost dead, trying to get her to tell him where her husband was. And the more she didn't tell him, the worse it got. After it was all over she wasn't the same beautiful woman we once knew, her face fell on one side, and she lost an eye." He paused before continuing.

"One day about a month later her husband came riding in on a horse and saw what had happened to his wife. He set back out and found that bounty hunter and killed him in front of an entire town. Word is he done it mid-afternoon in front of the sheriff. He came back to Marthasville and shortly after that the sheriff, and his deputies rode in and shot up the O'Connor house with both of them inside. They both shot back killing six of the 10 deputies, but ran out of ammo and had to turn themselves in.

Anyway, before they hung them both for the killings, they asked Mrs. O'Connor did she have any last words before they tied that rope around her neck. And the only thing she said is that she loved her husband wrong or right and would have done it that same if asked again. Sometimes I wonder what the nigger family would be like if we stuck to each other like Mrs. O'Connor stuck to her husband. I tell you, I don't think all of the evil things that have happened to our families would not be so often."

Minty looks at Matthew and starts to walk back toward the prison.

"Where are you going?"

"I'm going to risk my life in order to save your brother, I hope you are happy about that."

"I am not happy you have to risk your life, but I am grateful that you are going to try for me."

Minty looks at Matthew and shakes her head. She starts walking toward the jail and says out loud.

"I surely could have used a man like you years ago. I guess I am glad to see a little change in the Negro man."

Nathan is never the same.

Robert walks into the saloon like a new man. Because of all of the money and fame Robert and his band have been getting the past couple of weeks, Robert decided to buy himself and the band new clothes, so that their clothes fit the image they have in the town.

Robert walks pass a couple of the towns ladies and tips his hat in saying hello. The ladies smile and talk quietly amongst themselves as Robert walks away. Robert has become a well-liked and popular man in town from singing the songs that Nathan has wrote for him and his band.

He walks into the saloon and sees the owner cleaning the floors, it's pay-day, and Robert always comes bright and early so that he can collect what he is owed and gamble some away in the card games.

He sits at one of the card tables and smiles at the owner while shuffling a deck of cards and says, "We keep packing this saloon like we have the past week or so and you are going to have to sell me half of your saloon."

"You might be right. Hell, I served a man and his wife last night that came all the way from Clinton! That's over 50 miles away! They say that they heard about the new sound coming out of this town and wanted to hear it for themselves."

"Yes, sir we seem to be doing a hell of a job packing this place every night. Maybe instead of you selling me a piece of this place I should just open my own place up the road and run you out of business."

Bothered by Robert's comment, the saloon owner stops cleaning, turns to Robert and says, "Son, I have been in this-here town for over 10 years now. I have seen other saloon owners come and go. So what makes you think that you coming here singing would put me out of business?"

Robert sits back in the chair, looks around and says, "Well, the way I see it is you may have been open for the last 10 years but never have you packed this place like it has been the last couple of weeks. And I am almost sure that anyone that came into this town trying to open a saloon didn't have the entertainment to take the customers from you because they have known you for so long. But, see I have the talent, entertainment, and after today the start-up money to run you right out of here."

"Son, you may have the entertainment and the start up money, but you sure don't have enough talent. What you do have is a nigger that writes some of the best songs I have ever heard in my lifetime. But soon that will be over."

Robert

And what makes you say that?

"Well, I have noticed that you have been singing the same songs for the last couple of weeks, which means to me, either he has run out of songs or has stopped giving you guys new ones. And from the looks of him when I went out to the outskirts of town, because of all the beatings you fellas have put on him he probably has stopped talking."

"So, what does that mean to me?"

"Well, pretty soon the people here in town will stop wanting to hear the same songs over and over again. And eventually, they are going to start asking you for new ones to hear. Now, do you think you and your buddies are talented enough to write something like what that nigger fella has been writing for you?"

"I reckon that we could."

"Funny, I have talked to some of the people that come from the town you were in first, and they say some woman was with you before and she was the one singing and all while you guys just watched. They also said that the woman eventually got rid of you guys because you weren't helping her at all. Now, how do you go from being kicked out of a traveling band to becoming the headliner of a saloon in a matter of days? Good news is, just like the woman in Marthasville had to move on because people got tired of hearing the same old songs, you will too. And I will still be here running my saloon for another 10 years, watching traveling bands like you come and go."

"Is that so?"

"Yes, I believe it is. Now, here is the money that I owe you fellas for the last week. Make sure you save some of it for your travels soon and also do yourselves a favor and feed that nigger some food. Lord knows you're going to need him once your songs spread through the state. Won't be able to find a town that hasn't heard it for hundreds of miles then."

The saloon owner counts out the money owed to Robert and places it into an envelope. He then places the envelope on the table and says to Robert.

"Remember what I told you, get that nigger some food."

Robert leaves the saloon with money in hand thinking about what the saloon owner had said to him. As he walks past a small eatery, he slows down to really take in the sign. He looks back down the road to where the saloon stands, then walks right into the eatery. Moments later he returns to the street with a paper bag and proceeds to walk toward the campsite where Nathan has been for the last three weeks.

As Robert gets closer to the camp site he sees one of his band mates kicking Nathan who is chained on the side of the carriage they rode in on. Robert starts to jog toward his bandmate as he overhears the conversation.

"Those were perfectly good scraps and coffee beans for you to eat," said one of the bandmates.

Nathan replied, "I can't even swallow it, and I have seen what you and the other men do to it before you give it to me."

"Did you think we made enough money around here to feed ourselves and you too? Hell, you haven't wrote a new song since we have been here, I don't know why we just don't kill you now."

"Maybe if you guys started writing songs for yourselves, you wouldn't need to try to beat one out of me and just let me go."

"Nigger, you just bought yourself another beating. I'm going to whip you until you can't see straight."

Robert's band mate goes to take off the belt holding up his pants. He raises it as if he was about to strike Nathan with it, as Robert catches his arm. The band mate looks at Robert in confusion but eventually lowers his arm and walks away. Robert then walks over to Nathan and hands him the paper bag.

"What's this?"

"Steak, vegetables, and baked potatoes and some bread I think is in there. I also bought you a bottle of milk, I didn't think you drank being still a kid and all."

Nathan tears the bag open and starts to eat the food. He is so hungry that he stuffs his face full of food and almost chokes himself trying to drink the milk behind it. He looks up at Robert and says, "Why you being so nice to me all of a sudden?"

"Well, I have realized that even though me and my friends over there are good at music you have something that draws the people. Now, I want to apologize for how we treated you earlier, but you have to understand that I caught you kissing and spending time with my woman. Now, in other parts of the country, that kind of stuff will get you down right killed. So, what me and the boys have been doing to you for the past couple of weeks really wasn't that bad if you look at it. Anyway, I have an offer for you."

"Whats that?"

"Well, the town really likes the songs you have given us, and they pack the saloon every night to see us perform. But I know that soon they will stop coming if we don't come up with something else. So, let's say we pay you every week for creating new songs for us to sing. We will feed you, get you cleaned up, we may be able to find you a softer bed to sleep in. Now, of course, it won't be in the town because they don't serve niggers, but we can make this area as comfy as possible. What do you think? How much money will I make?"

"Well, how much money were you making down at that place you were working?"

"About five dollars a week."

"Well, I think that we can pay you 12 dollars a week on top of all that I have said. Is it a deal?"

Nathan thinks about the offer for a moment before he shakes his head agreeing with Robert. Robert knows Nathan has never seen that kind of money in his life but also knows that it isn't even a third of what they make in a weeks time from the saloon. Nathan looks up at Robert and says to him, "What about your friends?"

"Well, what about them?"

"Will they keep hitting me?"

"Now, remember, friend. That stuff was happening because of what you did. Now I could have very well just killed you. But I didn't because I realized I was fighting for a woman not worth fighting for."

"And all of this happened today?"

"Well, yes. Let's just say that I had a long talk with a man that told me to see the value in everything. So, I bought you some food and wanted to have this talk so that I could apologize for how we been treating you. Now, remember the bible says that you are supposed to forgive me. I mean what would Jesus have done?"

"He would have forgave."

"Well, then I reckon that you should do the same. Just like I have forgiven you for what you have done to me."

Chapter 18

Minty and Matthew - Going to get Mark from Prison

Minty and Matthew walk toward the prison without saying a word for half the way. Matthew, not sure if Minty is upset with him or not, from what he last said to her, continues to walk in silence until he can see the lights from the prison in the distance. Matthew hurries his steps to catch up to Minty as they go through the last set of thick trees before the prison. The building sits in the middle of an open field 10 yards in each direction. The building itself is made of brick, about 60 feet high and 50 yards in on each side. On top of the building are two very large smoke stacks that produce big clouds of smoke that disappear into the night air. In each corner of the building are big lights shining down onto the open field that are constantly moving. Nathan is worried about being caught by the guards and wants to ask Minty about his role in the rescue of his brother.

"So, what do you need me to do so that we can get him out of there?"

"Nothing."

"Look, I know you have been doing this for a long time, but you have to know you are going to need some help. I mean there is no way you are going to even get close to the building with those lights, and even if you do how are you going to even get close to it? How are you going to get in?"

"Well, I am going to just walk right in and get your brother out of jail."

"So let me understand what you are saying. You are just going to walk right into the building, and you and my brother are going to walk out holding hands?"

"No."

"I didn't think so."

"When we walk out, he will be holding the edge of my dress."

Matthew stands there for a moment and disbelief. Almost as if he is waiting for Minty to finish a joke that she is not telling. She continues to walk and then Matthew says, "So you are just going to walk in there with no weapons or anything? You do know that there are armed guards at the top of those towers with at least 20 more inside, guarding the prisoners. Do you have some type of gun or weapon I don't know about?"

"Yes, I do. Thank you for reminding me about that."
Minty turns back toward the last patch of woods they have just gotten to the edge of and softly whistles toward the trees. She does this three or four times before a chick comes out of the brush. The chicken looks around and then walks right up to Minty for her to pick it up. She picks it up and whispers something to it, and then Matthew says, "Is this your weapon?"

"Yes."

"We are about to get ourselves killed."

"No. This chicken and I are about to go and get your brother, and you are going to stay right here in the woods so that you are not seen. Do you understand?"

"I am supposed to trust you to bring my brother out of there with nothing other than a chicken to help you?"

"Yes."

Matthew realizes at this point he has to trust in Minty knowing something that he doesn't. So he agrees, and Minty walks over to the edge of the woods with the chicken. Matthew says a silent prayer to himself and shakes his head in disbelief as Minty speaks to the chicken again.

She puts the chicken down, and it starts to run into the open field as fast as it can. Once it gets to the middle of the field, both lights try to move to get a look at what it actually is. But the chicken seems to get away from the light. Once the chicken has taken the lights to the furthest point of its reach, Minty in Matthews disbelief walks right up to the side of the building and disappears. Matthew blinks and stares at the spot where his eyes lost Minty.

Once inside Minty walks through the jail as if she had been there before, timing every step the guards make so as to not be seen. By now most of the guards have run into the field to find out what the mysterious thing is running around. Minty walks right to the cell that Mark is being held in, but does not notice that Tiny is sitting in the cell next to them in the dark.

She looks in to see Mark and the old man talking and says to them both.

"Are you ready to leave here?"

"Oh hells yeah."

Mark quickly gets up and walks toward the cell door where Minty is unlocking it from the outside. She opens the door letting Mark out, but before she closes the door, she says again to Albert.

"Are you ready to leave here?"

Albert stands up and walks toward the cell door and puts his hand on top of Minty's hand pulling the jail door closed. He tears up and says to her, "You know I deserve to be here."

"And you have paid your time for that crime. You don't have to be here anymore if you don't want to."

"Well, I want to. The kid is clean. Before they could take his name and make a card, I shut the lights off. So, they don't even really know he was even here."

"Thank you, Albert. I will see you again soon."

Minty turns to Mark and says to him, "Hold on to the edge of my dress and don't let go no matter what. You do what I say, and you will walk out of here a free man do you understand."

"Yes, Ma'am."

Mark grabs hold of Minty's dress and begins to walk with her away from the cell. Just as they take the first two steps Tiny grabs Minty by the dress through the cell and says, "I want to be a free man too."

Minty moves the outer layer of her dress to the side to reveal a short barrel shot-gun. She takes the gun out and uses the butt of the gun to jam Tiny's arm into the cell he is in. Tiny let's go of Minty and says to her, "Bitch! You are going to pay for that! GUARDS!"

"And you call me a name?"

Minty jabs at Tiny's arm again, breaking it, and begins to walk outside of the jail. Every turn because of Tiny yelling out for attention is seconds from being discovered. Finally, Minty walks out of prison with Mark following closely behind holding her dress. Matthew stands in amazement as Minty walks up to him with his brother and says to him calmly but stern, "We have got to get out of here."

They all turn to run as one of the lights from the guard house catches them. The prison guards follow them into the woods with dogs in hand. They separate into three different directions and use what they have learned to run up the trees and disappear. The guards go to the spots' where they were and can't believe they have disappeared. Two guards let go of their dogs hoping they would be able to catch up to the three agents. However, eventually the dogs lose their scent and return to their owners confused. One guard looks at the other and says, "Did that just really happen?"

"They must be part monkey or something," said the other guard.

"Yea, monkeys or something."

The guards walk back toward the prison in confusion, looking back into the forest occasionally with their lanterns hoping to see something left by the three now escaped prisoners.

The day that congress knocked on the door, Mr. and Mrs. Lesure are sitting in their study enjoying each others company. Mrs. Lesure is sitting in her chair next to her husband's desk knitting a scarf for her husband for the upcoming winter. Mr. Lesure is reading his upcoming speech intently trying to fine tune it before his visit to congress in a few months.

Mrs. Lesure looks over at her husband, smiles and says, "I remember when we were younger and you were running for mayor. You had that same look on your face, so intent and focused. It's one of the things that made me fall in-love with you."

Mr. Lesure's eyes never leave his desk. He just moans toward his wife as if he heard her, but is in mid-thought. Finally, after writing his thought-down on a piece of paper, he looks over at her and says, "You know what, Elizabeth. I have been thinking about that very thing since I have returned. And I want to apologize to you."

"Why is that Mr. Lesure? You have given me everything I have ever hoped for and more the past 10 years. What could you ever be sorry for?"

"Well, I have been thinking a lot lately about my beginnings in politics. Just a young man standing on a soap box trying to be heard with hopes to change the world."

"And you have done that my love, you have turned this state into something people have finally been proud of since before the war. If it wasn't for you, the people in this state would have given up on this country a long time ago."

"I have done those things, but doing all of that I forgot about the most important things. I have been so busy with trying to save our race and this state that I forgot about saving our family."

"What do you mean?"

"Well, we have been saving the world, but we have never tried to save this family by having children. And I have come to the conclusion that I have been selfishly pursuing my goals and I never stopped to ask you what you may have wanted or even not wanted. I just want to say that I am sorry and if you would like to start a family now I would be glad to."

"I don't know what to say?"

"Just say yes, and we will start today."

Just as Mrs. Lesure goes to speak to her husband about what he has just asked, Emmet knocks on the outside of the open door and says, "Mr. Lesure, may I come in for a second?"

"Yes, Emmet. The Mrs. and I were talking so try to make it quick."

"I will, sir. I just got back from town and before I left, I stopped at the postmaster's office to see if you had any mail. Well, you did, sir, and it is a letter all the way from Washington. Well, at least that is what the postmaster says it says.

Mr. Lesure gets up and walks over to Emmet to see what he is talking about. He takes the letter from Emmett and opens it. He reads the first couple of sentences and starts to say to his wife, "It's a letter from Congressman Nelson. He says that there has been a breakout at the prison and he thinks that two of our niggers in town have something to do with it."

"So, what does he want you to do?"

"Nothing, he says that he is on his way here and will be staying with us while they do a census on the niggers here."

"What is a census?"

384

"Well, the first census was done in 1790 in this country. We were told it was to count the population of people in the country as a whole, but that isn't the case."

"So what do they do it for?"

"Well, around that time they were worried about the population of niggers in the country. Not only were the niggers themselves having babies for serving the white population. Some of the nigger owners started to have babies with the slaves as well. One day a French reporter came here and reported how he was outraged in his findings that good white folks had been mix breeding with the help. Which, we as a country didn't care about, but it got us thinking."

"About what?"

"Well, we started to wonder what would happen if the nigger out populated the white race in this country. So, they started the census so that they could keep track of how fast the nigger population was growing. That way if need be we could use different things to stop the growth."

"What do you mean stop the growth?"

"Well, the capital has been working on a new…. Emmet can you excuse us for a moment?"

"Yes, sir."

Emmet quickly leaves the room but stops shortly after walking out of the room so that he can hear the rest of the conversation.

"They are working on a new drug that can help slow down the births of nigger children in this country. They are calling it Syphilis. It's an infection that has been in the world for a long time, except here in America. We are starting to control it, actually learning to make it. Well, they are thinking about using the infection on niggers to curb the population a little. They said that they are using it to see the effects of progression, but that's just so people don't get too sensitive about the subject."

Emmet overhears what Mr. Lesure is saying and quickly leaves to get back to the lake and tell the Professor. Meanwhile, Mrs. Lesure is listening to her husband in disbelief.

"I can't believe what I am hearing."
"Well, believe it, my dear. There is nothing more important in this country than preserving the white race."

"I see, well when will the Congressman be here?"

"Well, this letter left Washington three days ago. So according to this letter he will be here tomorrow."

"Well, in that case, we need to hurry and get our house in order. There are so many things that need to be done."

"I agree. Let us start right away."

Chapter 19

"Who was that man?"

The twins are walking through the forest in the early morning trying to get closer to the town their friend is being held captive. Mark thinks about his time in the penitentiary and the old man that taught him so much in so little time. He remembers what Minty asked him before she closed the prison door and realizes through all the excitement that she knows him somehow. He slows down so that he can talk to Minty for a moment before they hide for the day.

"I just wanted to thank you for saving me back there. It had started to sink in that I was going to be there for a while, and when you came walking in, I was surprised but very thankful."

"Well, thank your brother because I did it for him, not you. I would never risk my life for the hardheaded."

"I understand, but I wanted to thank you anyway. May I ask you a question?"

"You slowed down to talk to me so I guess you might as well."

"Back at the prison, I thought you came to get me. But, when you turned to Albert and asked him was he ready to go yet, I figured you knew him. But how?"

"What do you mean?"

"Well, he has been in there for the past 30 years, and he says no one has ever visited. Yet, you talk to him as if you know him."

Minty looks at Mark and keeps walking. She looks away into the morning sky before she starts to tell Mark, the story of an old friend.

"Years ago when this organization started Albert and I were lovers. We were actually going to get married until things got a little messy in our fight for freedom."

"I don't understand."

"Well, most of this younger generation has no clue about the people that died for them just to get a glimpse of freedom. See, there were all types of rebellions going on in this country in the day. Albert and I didn't join until the Nat Turner revolt in 1831. But as kids, we would read what the white man had to say. We would read about George Boxley and Amistad and wonder if we could ever be apart of it. Even then we were breaking the law, but too young to even know why we just did what they told us to do and played as if we couldn't read when we were asked. Told Master Ross that we needed to use the old newspapers for blinds in the slave houses. And he would also rent us to other plantations to work the fields, but what he didn't know is that some of the plantation owners were abolitionists and would send us to different places to help the cause. See, white folks at

391

the time would help you organize but at the end of the day they still white folks. Anyway, one day Albert and I decided that we were going to sign up for a real field mission. This wasn't no retrieve chickens to feed us better or taking Mrs. Ross to the other side of the plantation so that we could sneak back onto the field, no sir. We got sent down to Virginia from Maryland to help a young preacher man who believed in a more violent way. So, the summer of 1831 we set out for Virginia and met this man in the woods with six other people that he knew. He talked about killing the masters and their families in order to gain power, I didn't particularly care for what he was saying, but Albert felt that it was the only way. He decided that he was going to help the preacher man instead of helping bring the slaves back to Maryland and possibly to Canaan like we were told to do." He paused before continuing.

"Well, I did what I was told to do, and Albert went with the young preacher into the houses of the slave owners. Albert once told me later that everything was going fine because they were just going to kill the masters and their wives. That was until the daughter of the plantation came into the room, and

392

Albert killed her. It started the rest of the men to do the same at every house they went to. Albert didn't mean to kill the child, but she scared him walking into the bedroom where her mother and father had slept. After they left the house one of the men realized they had left a baby alive in the house and the preacher sent Albert and two of his men back to the house to finish what they had started. Albert told the two men he would go in and kill the baby but didn't. Instead, he ran out of the back of the home and dropped the baby off near a home halfway back to Maryland." He took another breath.

"Anyway, for years Albert and I would help in different missions to free our people. From the Cherokee Nation revolt to John Brown's raid, we were there for the fight and able to get out alive without capture. Well, one day Albert was caught talking to a group of Negro men in public and sentenced to 13 years in prison. But because of the guilt, he has for what he had done he just stays there."

"Wait, are you telling me that old man can walk out of there any time he wanted to?"

"Yes, I guess even when doing the right thing, sometimes the mind doesn't let you forget it was the wrong thing. I guess we should camp here before it gets any lighter outside."

"Yea, I guess we should. After hearing that I need to get some sleep."

Chapter 20

After walking for almost two days Minty, Mark, and Matthew finally come to a crossroad. They are not sure which way to go seeing that they have been two weeks behind freeing Mark. And they are not sure which road to take for fear of losing Nathan further away from Marthasville.

"So, which way should we go, Minty?"

"I'm not sure. What did that lady Mrs. Debbie say before we left?"

"She said that they were headed to Marionville, which is about five miles that way." As Matthew says this to Minty, he points left to the east. "But, we are behind about two weeks so they could be headed toward the Carolina's by now."

"And if they are headed that way it will take us to far away from Marthasville. We have very important business to take care of, and we can't afford to take up any more time. You two are going to have to make a decision on what you want to do."

"What do you mean?"

"You two are going to have to decide if your friend is more important than your own lives. The further we go away from Marthasville the less help, we will have if need be. I am the only person to leave the south and survive on their own, and I will not allow you to get me killed for your problems."

"So what are you saying?"
"I'm saying that if you are going to continue on with this journey with my help, you are going to have to pray he is still in Marionville. Because if he is not, this journey is over."

Just then, they hear a small child walking from the direction of Marionville singing a song. As the boy gets closer to the fork in the road where Minty, Matthew, and Mark are standing, they start to make out the words that the little girl is singing.

"The days we spend

The times we share

All alone at this piano

Wishing you were there

But through it all I sing out loud

Knowing that you are listening

And hope that you are proud."

Minty walks out of the brush and scares the little girl who is carrying fish she caught out of the lake. Minty says to her, "Excuse me, little girl, can I ask you a question?"

"Yes, ma'am?"

"Me and those guys over there heard you singing, and we really liked the song.

Where did you learn that song?"

"My, Paw. He works as a dishwasher in town, and he said he heard it from a new band that came to town."

"How long have you been singing that song?"

"I would say about a week ago. My paw came home every night singing that song to my sister and I."

"It's a very pretty song. Can you tell us where you're from?"

"Yes, we are from a town about five miles from here called Marionville. I am on my way back there so that I can start cooking for my family. Would you like to walk with me?"

"Well, here is the thing. We are hiding from some people and can't be seen. So, we will walk with you along the forest line. Just remember, that if someone stops you and asks, you are by yourself."

"Okay, so why are you hiding?"

"Well, we are playing a game, and we don't want them to find us."

"I know that game! Me and my sisters play that all the time. Don't worry I am a great hider and secret keeper."

"Okay, we are walking right next to you in the forest."

Robert is sitting in a clothing store with one of his band mates. In the background, Nathan is being fit for a suit that he will be wearing. Robert's band member stands in disbelief at the fact of a nigger being fit for an expensive suit. And part jealous because he himself does not own a suit of that quality.

After watching in silence until it becomes too much to handle, he says to Robert, "I don't understand why you have been treating him so well the last couple of weeks. He isn't even apart of the group! Yes, he writes songs, but that doesn't give him a better position than the men that have been with you for the last six years. He wasn't there when we were getting chased out of bars and scraping for money to buy food. I have to say I don't like how he is being put on a higher priority. After all, he is still a nigger."

Robert looks at John and laughs silently as he ushers him to the front door of the store. They walk outside, and Nathan takes out a package that contains pre-rolled cigarettes and offers one to John. John takes one and waits for Robert to light it with a gold cigar lighter. They both take a pull from their cigarettes as Robert starts to talk.

"You know, there was a time where I didn't think we were going to make it. How long have we been friends, John?"

"Hell, since our mothers moved into that shack at the age of seven or so. We are 35 now, so for a pretty long time."

"Exactly, and you know I wouldn't trade that for the world. Did you like living the way we did?"

"You know I didn't, the working day in and out for little of nothing. I remember some nights we didn't eat so that our sisters could have a meal. Those were some hard times. Now that I think about it, isn't that the reason we started this band?"

"It was so that we could possibly make enough money so that we wouldn't have to starve anymore. You know, I hated to see our mothers crying because our fathers didn't want to be there. I dreamed about the day that I could provide for them, and without an education, I didn't have that many choices. I only stayed with the music because I didn't have any other talents."

"Who are you telling? Remember, how much trouble we would get into for not picking the cotton for the day. I still can't believe you would get into the sack so that it would weigh out the right way. But, boy, when it got back to Mr. Harmon for the final weigh and was at least 20 pounds short, our mothers would have a fit!"

Robert laughs and says to John.
"I remember that I still have switch marks on my legs so that I will never forget. So once we got to our teenage years, we set out to become one of the best bands ever. We had some highs, a lot of lows. I even got married in the process and lost my wife to the man we are now putting in an expensive suit."

"Which is why I don't understand what we are doing here with him. After all, we have been through."

"Tell me, John. How much money have you sent your mother and family in the last couple of weeks while the nigger has been with us?"

"More than I have ever sent in the last couple of years."

"And the reason for all of us being able to provide for our families and send our sisters to school is because of that well-dressed nigger in that store. My youngest sister will be attending school, and she is the first one in our family. I will do anything to make sure that happens, and at least one of them makes it out of what we hated so much, even if that means working with a nigger."

"I understand now. But, you're talking about letting him perform with us now. It was one thing for him to write a couple of songs but for him to be on the same stage with us is crazy!"

"He will not be on the same stage. We will perform our songs first, and then for the closing of the show, we will let him perform behind a curtain. The crowd will think it's a part of the show, so they won't think twice about not being able to see him. Then we will also have a new song to take with us to the next town because I think our time here is done."

"I like how you think, Robert. It's no different than the nigger on the plantations picking the cotton. As long as the cotton is ours and not theirs, who cares?"

"Right, and this time the cotton comes in the form of bills."

Robert pulls a bill fold out full of crisp bills. They both laugh and hug each other as Robert opens the door to the store and says to John, "You know what, you do need a new suit. Let's go ahead and get you one."

Mr. and Mrs. Lesure sit waiting on the arrival of the Governor. Mr. Lesure paces back and forth, nervous about his visitor's arrival. He knows that one approval from the Governor will put him in a great position of power and hopes that he has the best time of his life.

Mrs. Lesure sits patiently sewing while she watches her husband in his nervous state. She knows how important this is to him and wishes him all the best. She then thinks about Carolyn and wonders if her relationship with her is something

404

that shouldn't be. Is being with a woman not natural? Who gives people the right to judge who I love?

Just then, Emmet comes to the foyer of the house and announces the arrival of Mr. Smith. Mr. Smith is a very large man with a long, curly, gray mustache. He wears thin rimmed glasses and speaks in a proper voice, "Good evening, Mr. Lesure. I tell you the ride from the capital was horrible! We have a new driver, and I think this is the first time he has ever driven a carriage in his life!"

"Welcome, Mr. Smith I am so glad that you made it. We received your letter just days ago, and we have been preparing for your arrival ever since. Let my servant get those bags for you."

"Thank you, my good sir. All I need now is a good meal, wine, and a fine cigar. And maybe if you can arrange a maid to come by my room after I retire. Preferably a Negro one."

Mr. Lesure looks around nervously in response to Mr. Smith's comment.

"Oh, don't act so surprised. It's the same question you asked me when you came to visit."

"Yes, it was. I'll make sure I get that arranged for you."

Mr. Smith moves from the side of Mr. Lesure to directly in front of him with a smile as if he has just learned something.

"Well look at you now."

"What do you mean?"

Mr. Smith responds in a low voice so not to be heard, "Just a little over a month ago you were standing in the grand entrance of the capital telling us stories of fornication and spirits. You even told us of a child that you had fathered with a servant years ago that works at the nigger store. You talked so freely as if you were just like the rest of us. And now you are cowering at the conversation, which tells me one thing. That Mrs. Lesure does not know about all of this."

"She knows, we just don't talk about it."

"It's none of my business anyway, I am sorry that I pried."

"Don't worry about it, what would you like to do first now that you are here?"

"I would love to take a bath. All the dirt and insects along the way make me want to throw everything I have on into the fire."

"Well come on, I will have one of the maids start you a bath."

Chapter 21

Minty, Matthew, and Mark finally reach the town Marionville with little daylight left.

They thank the little girl as she skips toward her home in the small village.

Standing at the edge of the village Minty reads a sign that says "Niggers not allowed after nightfall. Must be working." They all look into the town and realize that all of the negroes are walking out of the main part of town and into the villages that sit on the far side of town. Matthew looks at Mark and says to him, "Well, I wouldn't think that they would bring Nathan inside the town anyway. It will be easier for us to get him back with one or two people watching over him than the entire band."

"That's true. All we will have to do is get to the other side of town and find their camp, then we head home."

Just as Mark is saying this, Matthew sees Robert rushing Nathan into the back alley of the saloon with a white blanket over his head.

"Well, so much for the easy way. It's only one way now."

"About time, Minty I knew you were going to do something. So what is it? Are we just going to bust in and take him out of there?"

"No."

"Okay. Then what? We are going to sneak in, and when the time is right we are just going to jump out kick some people in the stomach and walk out with him?"

"Nope."

"Then what in tarnation are we going to do?"

"WE gone get a job, and we gone be working."

Minty walks toward the sign in the alley that reads "Kitchen help wanted. Dishwashers and servers needed." Mark continues to stand there as Matthew walks by him. Mark turns and looks at his brother and says, "I am guessing you are going to get a job as well."

"Not like we don't have the skill. We help Mrs. Debbie all the time at her place, and it's probably better pay."

"How you figure?"

"Cause Mrs. Debbie never paid us."

Matthew continues to walk behind Minty toward the alley and Mark, realizing that his brother has a point and decides to go along with the plan.

Inside the saloon behind the stage, Robert and Nathan are talking about what has to happen in order for the night's performance to work. The owner stands guard at the stage

411

entrance, so no one comes and sees what is happening. Robert says to Nathan.

"Okay, after we finish our set tonight we will leave room for one more song. You will have to perform behind the curtain because if they see you right away, they won't give you a chance."

"Right."

"Then after you finish your song we will raise the curtain and show them who is really writing all these songs. By then they will love you, and everything will be fine. Hey, how did you like the suit?"

"I have never had clothes like this in my entire life. The nicest thing I ever had was my Sunday suit for church, and that was my brothers before I ever was born."

"See, and if you stay with me, you will be able to buy more suits than you could ever imagine. And maybe more, you may be able to own your own land someday."

"You think so? I would really like to do something for my family. We don't really have much back home, and I would want them to at least have something. Maybe my baby sister could be the first in our family that could go to school."

Robert looks over Nathan's shoulder at the owner as he smiles from Nathan's comment. Robert then says to Nathan, "If we pull this off and start to record your songs you can have anything you want. But, to think your sister should go to school is a little bit crazy don't you think?"

"Well, we been told that we could do just about as much as you can, Robert. And I think it's a good thing for not only my sister, but the future of my family."

"Okay, Nathan. Whatever you say. Hey, go ahead and get ready for your song, before you know it we will be finishing our set."

"You are right! I need to rehearse the new song I have been working on." Nathan walks over close to the piano that sits behind the stage and lightly plays the keys to the new song he is going to sing. Robert stands next to the saloon owner, who says to Robert, "You know there is no way we are going to open that curtain. The only reason I am even allowing you to pull this off is because you said you would cut me into the recording deal."

"And that offer still stands. When he finishes his song we will escort him right out of the back door, tell him some story about the people not being ready for something different and move on to the next city. That way while we are traveling and playing we can make some money elsewhere."

In the kitchen of the saloon stand Minty, Matthew, and Mark. Matthew and Minty are dressed as waiters, while Mark has been given the job of dishes and trash.

"Well look at it this way. This is exactly what you would have been doing back at Mrs. Debbie's. This was the best outfit for you." Minty laughs to herself.

"Look, let's just get Nathan out of here so that we can head home. It looks like he will be playing the piano behind the curtain for the band. I must say, that is the closest anyone of us has been to a white stage."

"Amen to that."

"So, I guess the plan is to wait until there is a song he doesn't play. Minty and I will go get him and walk him out of the back door of the stage. It will already be a question of where we went to, so you are going to have to stay and finish your job until the saloon closes."

"What! Are you telling me I am going to have to wash dishes for the rest of the night?"

"You did say you wanted to help your friend, well this is what needs to be done. Now, let's just get to work before anyone catches us standing around."

Minty and Matthew walk away while Mark continues to clean the dishes. As they enter the main dining area, Minty says to Matthew quietly.

"Why didn't you tell your brother he could just leave when we finally walk Nathan out of here? It will put us at least two hours behind on getting back to Marthasville."

"Yea, but I figure all the problems he gave us by getting arrested a couple weeks back it would be fun to watch him finish his job."

"You know, that would be fun to see."

Minty and Matthew walk out of the kitchen and into the main area of the saloon where it is packed from wall-to-wall with people talking, laughing and drinking. One woman sits in the middle of the saloon right in front of the stage. A heavy set lady that has an appetite that matches, drinks and eats while waiting on the show to begin.

Robert sees her through the curtain and cringes at the sight of her. He looks over at John who is laughing in his hand trying to control his outbursts.

"Why is it that you laugh every time she comes to our shows?"

"Because not only is she one of the biggest reasons we have been successful in this town, she also is the biggest contributor to our band by being the biggest supporter for buying up most of the seats in the front area."

"So why is that funny?"

"Well, because she is also your biggest fan. And quite frankly, the biggest person here."

John can no longer hide is emotions and laughs uncontrollably and loudly at Robert. Robert, however, is not laughing and instead takes a long stiff drink of Green River Whisky right from the bottle.

"No matter how much of that stuff you drink she is not going to get any smaller." Robert says laughing. As he passes John the bottle.

"Shut up! That's why I am so glad we are getting out of here after tonight. By the time we come back around here, she will be gone from heart failure of some sort."

"Me too. Hey, I just wanted you to know that you were right about Nathan."

"What do you mean?"

"Well, I have actually been talking to him the last couple of days, and he has been helping with my drumming as well. He isn't a bad kid. I just hope he realizes where ever we go he still will be a nigger. And ain't much we can do about the rules, you know?"

"John, we never made the rules. And the way I see it we are helping him reach the ears of people who would have never listened to him by giving him a chance. Truth is I don't see any niggers opening up saloons and recording companies for him to perform in. And I don't want to see his talents go to waste, but for that, we will have to get something in return. My wife made a comfortable home for herself before she got rid of us, but that won't last long. Remember this has nothing to do with niggers vs whites. It has everything to do with the rich and the poor."

As Robert finishes his sentence, they both hear the saloon owner talking to the crowd, which is their cue to get in place for the show.

Minty and Matthew are serving food and drinks to the other customers as they notice Nathan taking his place behind the curtain for the show.

Mark gives a silent head signal to Minty who is standing by the bar waiting on drinks she is serving. She looks in the direction that Matthew is pointing and sees Nathan behind the curtain as well.

Just then, one of the other waiters is being harassed by a customer that gets into his way purposely. He moves out of the way so that the man can walk by and as the waiter tries to pass him the customer trips him, laughs and says, "Looks like you will be cleaning up too!"

The entire saloon laughs as Matthew heads toward the waiter. Minty calls to him as he passes her and she shakes her head no in disapproval. Matthew then goes back to what he was originally doing while the waiter picks himself up and continues on.

Matthew is angry that he could not help the waiter. He circles the man who did it, a couple of times in between tables just so that he could remember his face.

He stops and almost-stares at the man and does not notice Minty standing right in front of him. She puts her hand on his shoulder to get his attention, as he looks at her directly in her eyes, she says quietly, "Sometimes the violence you feel in your heart is justified. But, sometimes it happens so that you can lose focus on the bigger picture. You fight now and everything that we have worked for will be nothing but become a picnic for them when they string us up over lunch. Always remember the only safe time to fight is when it doesn't put the people you are trying to defend in a bad place, okay?"

Matthew looks over at the waiter who moments ago was embarrassed by the man now smiling and acting as if it never happened. Matthew looks back at Minty and says to her, "Why don't we ever stand up for ourselves?"

"Because it's hard to find people who are willing to risk it all and stand with us. It's the reason why they have always won."

Matthew looks back over at the waiter and slowly untightens his fist. He realizes what Minty is saying to him, calms down, and goes back to work. The saloon owner who is still talking to the crowd getting ready to introduce the band finishes a joke and finally says, "Okay, without further ado, here is the band you have been waiting for. Here are Robert Swederski and his band of brothers!"

The crowd erupts into applause as the main curtain opens and Robert appears with his band. Robert shakes the hand of the saloon owner and says over the microphone, "Let's thank William again for letting us play in this wonderful saloon. Remember, your only job tonight is to enjoy the music and to keep the bartender busy." The crowd applauds.

"We are going to start with some songs that you guys have heard already before and then get into some new music the band, and I have been working on. So without any more talking, here are my band of brothers!"

Music starts to play, and the crowd really starts to get into it. The heavy lady in the middle of the room gets up to start dancing. She walks up to the front of the stage where Robert is singing as he walks back and forth on the stage trying not to make eye contact. The crowd starts to dance to the music, and the party starts. The bartenders are busy pouring the drinks and talking to the people at the bar. Even the waiters start to dance while walking back and forth to the tables serving food and drinks. The saloon owner stands at the far end of the bar watching the patrons with a smile.

The kitchen help even hears the music, and Mark cracks a smile because the song that is being played is the song Nathan would play during his fights at Mrs. Debbie's place in Marthasville. He taps the guy next to him on the shoulder who is also washing dishes and says, "Hey, my friend wrote that song."

"Really? You know Mr. Robert?"

"No, my friend Nathan wrote that song."
"You mean the young nigger boy that helps them bring in the instruments?" "Yea, that's him!"

The dishwasher looks at Mark with a face of disbelief, "There is no way your friend wrote that song."

"And why is that?"

"Because niggers don't write songs like that."

Robert and his band continue to play music, playing different songs that Nathan has taught them along the way. Robert finally goes into the song that helped Mark, Matthew and Minty find Nathan. He goes into the beginning of the song with the same lyrics, but a different way of singing it, which Mark and Matthew do not remember.

"The days we spend

The times we share

All alone at this piano

Wishing you were there

But through it all I sing out loud

Knowing that you are listening

And hope that you are proud."

"What the hell is that?"

"That is what we like to call music here in Marionville."

"You are right because I would never listen to anything like that."

Robert finishes the song, and the crowd erupts in applause. Robert's fan club of women stand and cheer as his number one fan stands in front of all of them so that she is seen by Robert. Robert smiles brightly until he sees her and then abruptly stops smiling. He then waves at the rest of the crowd and then walks off the stage while saying to the crowd, "We are going to take a quick break. When we come back we have a new act we would like to introduce here in Marionville!"

Robert walks backstage to talk to Nathan before he goes up to the balcony where he will be performing. He walks over to Nathan and says, "Are you ready for your debut?"

"I think so. I'm so nervous it's hard to tell."

"Don't be nervous , just remember to play like you always do."

"Okay."

"Oh, and you're going to have to wear this while you are performing."

Robert hands Nathan a blond, straight-haired wig. Nathan looks down at the wig and then back at Robert.

"What is that for?"

"It's for you."

"Why would I need a wig?"

"So that no one knows that you are…"

"A nigger?!"

"When you say it that way it sounds bad. But, the truth is that audience isn't ready for what you have to bring. All we have to do is let them hear what you have to offer and they will buy it by the boatload. By then it won't even matter what you look like, we will be so far from here that it will be a thing of the past. We can change the world by doing this, and all I need you to do is

427

wear this wig for one night. You said you wanted your sister to get into school, right?"

"Yes, more than you could ever imagine."

"Well, here is your chance to make that happen."

Robert hands Nathan, the wig and Nathan, puts it on. Robert turns his head and wipes his mouth from dryness. He takes a deep breath and then says to Nathan.

"Now, all you have to do is play the songs we have been practicing, and we will leave for another town. I am hearing that they are trying to put live songs on this contraption and people can buy them and play it in their homes without you even being there. We will make a fortune and will be able to do whatever it is that we want. You just have to trust me. Just go up there and play the songs."

That's what I will do, but I have been working on some sound changes."

"Sound changes?"

"Yes, they just sound a little different than before. I guess you are just going to have to trust me."

Nathan goes up to the balcony and waits for Robert to introduce him. Robert thinks about what Nathan has just said right before the saloon owner walks up to him and says, "Are you sure this is going to work?"

"Yes, we give him 10 minutes and no matter where he is in the song we will cut him off."

"Okay."
Robert walks over to the front of the stage and introduces Nathan to the crowd. "Are you guys enjoying yourselves so far?"

The crowd erupts in applause for what they have heard so far.

"Thank you, and we want you guys to know that we appreciate all the love you have shown us the last couple of weeks. We will be moving on to another town soon, so we wanted to leave you guys and gals with something new."

We have a musician that we would like you to hear, but he is a very shy person. So we will be performing behind the curtain from the balcony. Ladies and gentlemen, without further ado, here is our friend Nathan.

The stage goes dark as the light adjusts behind Nathan toward the crowd in the balcony where Nathan is sitting. Minty and Matthew look up into the balcony to see Nathan wearing the wig and shake their heads. Matthew can't believe that his friend is doing this in order to play for people that would never normally listen to him. Nathan starts by singing a slow ballot.

"Riding from town to town

Trying to find that new sound.

Playing late nights, trying to find something new

Future looks bright, but all I can think about is you

Wrong or right, I have to do what I have to do

Sitting up here so I can sing this song

But should I be here, what's right or wrong?"

Nathan begins to play a more upbeat song with the same lyrics that gets the crowd involved. People start dancing, drinking more and having a wonderful time. Robert and the rest of the band look on, and John walks over to the drums and starts playing along with Nathan. Robert and the saloon owner look at the crowd. However, Robert isn't happy that the crowd is responding so positively.

"I will let him play one more song, and we will close out for the night."

"Do you hear that crowd? That music has made this bar more money than it ever has, even more money then when it was just you guys! Keep him playing!"

Robert bites his tongue about what the saloon owner has just said. He looks over at the silhouette of Nathan in the balcony, then looks at the crowd. Even the heavy set woman that is usually his biggest fan now is staring at the balcony eating trying to figure out who is behind the curtain. Robert then looks over at his drummer and friend John who seems to be having a great time playing behind Nathan. Robert looks over at the rope next to him and sees that it will let the curtain, which is hiding Nathan fall to the ground. He looks around and then walks off to look for something.

In the kitchen, Mark stands with the rest of the dishwashers and says to them, "Now that's what I call music. You guys hear that? That's my friend out there."

"First off, there is no way a white man is going to call you friend."

432

"Well, he isn't white he is a Negro like you and I."

The entire dishwashing crew stands up and laughs at Mark for what he has just said. Mark looks at them as if he is trying to figure out why they are laughing.

"You know, boy. You may be a little crazy, but this is the most laughs we have had back here in months! You should be on stage with your friend!"

The entire kitchen erupts in laughter again. Some of the guys pat Mark on the back as if they are really being entertained.

The party is still going and by now everyone in the band except for Robert is enjoying Nathan's set. Robert has now walked down the hallway and entered one of the dressing rooms where a sharp throwing knife sits on top of a carnival colored box. He goes to it and runs his finger over it as if to see if it was sharp, and then walks casually back out of the dressing room.

The band is having a wonderful time playing along side of Nathan. People are even coming in from off the street who were once in other bars.

Everyone is having a good time as Robert walks slowly toward the rope that holds the curtain masking Nathan. He looks around to see if anyone is watching and then starts to cut the rope. He gets half way through the rope when John standing from behind him says, "What are you doing?"

"Why aren't you out there playing with the rest of the guys?"

"Well, I was taking a break to come and find you to see if you would like to join us, that Nathan can really play a tune. But I see now that you may not agree with Nathan playing here anymore. Can I ask you why?"

Robert pauses a moment looking down at the knife and then at the half cut rope. He looks over at John and says, "I have worked my whole life in music and finally got the chance to be someone. I sacrificed my home, my wife, and now my friends to a nigger who can hold a tune. I made him who he is, and this is what he does to me, to us? I'm going to show this nigger that he is only what I allow him to be."

Robert turns to the rope to finish cutting. The rope gives, and the curtain falls as Nathan continues to play. The crowd inside the saloon is not paying attention to the curtain and continues to drink and socialize. The only person that sees what is happening is the saloon owner. He looks around and slowly walks out of the main area so that he is not accused of hiring Nathan to play.

Robert and John creep out of the saloon through the back walking past Mark in a hurry. Mark sees the tail end of Johns jacket as the door closes behind him. Mark looks out into the main hall as a busboy walks out to retrieve plates and sees Matthew pacing and looking upward toward the balcony.

Matthew instantly sees Nathan exposed from behind the curtain and goes into a small panic, but Minty grabs his attention by walking over to him and says, "Just be patient. They haven't recognized that they can see him yet."

Just then one of the people in the crowd says, "He is a nigger!"

The crowd hears him and continues to dance and talk. But as the seconds pass each person starts to look up into the balcony to see a singing Nathan with a wig on. Nathan continues to play as the crowd gets silent and the band runs out of the room. Nathan finally notices that everyone can see him and stops playing the music.

"Well, I think they have finally noticed."

"Get that nigger!"

A crowd of men run up the stairs into the balcony as Minty and Matthew scale the wall by using the light fixtures to get to Nathan first. They then jump back down with Nathan and run into the kitchen with the crowd of men closely behind. The rest of the people in the main room stand in silence as they realize that they have been listening to a Negro. The only thing that breaks the silence is the bartender whistling the melody of the song Nathan was just playing.

Minty and Matthew have just run through the kitchen with Nathan and are feet from the back door when one of the men from the main room chasing them yells out, "Grab them, niggers!"

One of the dishwashers goes to grab Matthew who is the last of the three to get to the back door. Mark sees this and responds by grabbing the man by his arm and throwing him into the mob chasing after them. Mark then runs out the back door and pulls it shut, but the men are on the other side of the door trying to get in. Matthew comes back to help his brother hold them back for a moment, but realizes that it will not last for long. Mark looks at Matthew and says, "Brother, you are going to have to go with them, and I will catch up as soon as I can."

"I am not leaving you here to fight alone. If we are going to fight we are going to do it together."

Matthew yells over to Minty and Nathan, "Minty, take Nathan into the woods, and we will meet you guys there! Hurry!"

Minty without a word or hesitation runs through the back alley with Nathan toward the dark woods, east of the town. Matthew and Mark continue to hold the door shut until Nathan and Minty are out of sight. Once they were gone, Mark looks at his brother and says, "You ready for a little fun?"
"I think so."

"Well, just remember when we let this door go, it's no longer practice."

"Yes, I know."

Mark and Matthew finally let the door go and step back into the alleyway. The men finally realize that the door is free and calmly open it to see the twins waiting for them. One of the men says, "Well, boy. It looks like you made the wrong choice about not running."

"Well, let's find out and see."

The men walk out into the alley and surround the twins. One of them sticks a broom inside the door handle so that no one can come in or out. Matthew and Mark smile at each other as Mark says out loud.

"Thank you for keeping the fight even for us."

The twins proceed to beat each man up together. It looks like a rehearsed dance that none of the men can understand or counter. Finally, after seeing what has happened to the other men who came out of the saloon, the last man pulls a gun and says, "That's enough!"

The man goes to shoot at the twins who are too far away to defend themselves from the attack. A shot rings out, and both of the twins close their eyes hoping that the man missed.

They both look down at themselves, then each other. And then notice the man is barely standing with the gun about to fall over. They look behind them and see Minty with her long dress pulled up on one side and a short barreled shotgun in her hand.

The twins look at her because this entire time she has never made mention of the gun. She looks at both of them and says, "I did it because it was necessary."

"Thank you. Let's get out of here, I think I hear them coming!"

They all go running toward the forest line where Nathan is waiting for them. Once they get into the treeline, the mob comes from the side of the building, and they are nowhere to be found. One of the men looks-at the bodies on the ground, and the man who had been shot. He then looks down at the footprints left by Mark and Matthew and says, "They went that-a-way," said one of the men.

The now growing crowd starts to walk toward the entry of the forest where they suspect the group has gone.

Matthew and Mark catch up to Minty and Nathan a quarter of a mile into the forest. Minty is standing behind Nathan with her hand still firmly over the gun. She looks around to make sure it's the twins who are trying to catch up and then slowly drops the gun back under her dress. As the twins get closer, they notice Minty shaking her head at whatever Nathan is telling her. They walk to get closer to them and can overhear some of what Nathan is saying.

"And the way all those white folk were just dancing to my songs. It's what I have been dreaming about all my life, something like that will never happen again. Did you guys see that crowd?"

"The one that was standing in disbelief or the one that was trying to kill you?" Nathan looks at Matthew and carefully thinks about what he is going to say next.

"Listen, I understand what you guys did for me, and I thank you but let's look at the bright side of all of this. I may have just been the first Negro to ever play in front of a white crowd. Do you know what that will do for Negro music? We will be able to play all the big ballrooms across the country!"

"Maybe, but at what cost?"

Just then Robert and the rest of his band mates come within feet of Matthew trying to escape the town, before they are found and put on trial for bringing Nathan into a public place. Nathan sees Robert and the rest of the band walking by and before they can say something to him he says, "Robert, over here!"

Minty, Matthew, and Mark all turn and disappear into the shadows of the forest. Nathan looks around to see that they are gone, but before he can address it Robert says to him, "You got away? I thought they were going to try to kill you."

"They were, but some of the waiters helped me escape before they could get a hold of me."

"I am so glad they didn't catch you. We were hoping you would get away so that we could go on to other towns and keep the music going. Did you see how that crowd responded to you?"

"I was just telling my friends about that. It was the best feeling I have ever had."

"That's why you should come with us. That crowd of people is on its way into the forest to find you. We can hide you in our rig and get you out of here. They didn't even suspect us, they thought it was the saloon owner that put you up to it."

Just then Minty comes from behind the tree she had been standing, to say something to the both of them while the twins stay hidden. She came out and surprised Robert by saying, "So, is that the reason you cut the rope that held the curtain up in front of Nathan?"

Robert reaches for his gun but stops when he noticed Minty's shotgun already out and pointed in his direction. Robert moves his hand away from the holster on his left hip and puts his hands up. He steps back away from Nathan and says to Nathan.

"I didn't know that you weren't alone. I am not a threat to you if that is what you are worried about. Nathan and I are friends."

"Is that why you cut the rope for people to see what he looked like?" Nathan looks over at Robert as if to be waiting on an answer.

"Yes, I was the one that cut the rope, but I did it for your own good."
Mark comes from behind one of the trees and goes to stand next to Minty. He looks at her, reaches for her shotgun and says, "Let me kill him."

Robert starts to talk faster in hopes to get himself out of the situation.

"I did it because, Nathan, you weren't ready for what was about to happen. You don't understand what it takes to be with that kind of power, but I can help you with that."

"How can you help me get those people back listening to my music?"

"There is a new machine that has come out in the past couple of years called a Phonograph. It can record sound of any kind, including music, and people are starting to buy them to be used at home. We can record your songs on this machine and make thousands of dollars by just selling the recorded music. Your music will be heard in homes across the country. All you have to do is trust me."

Nathan looks over at Minty and Mark and then back Robert.

"So, you are saying my music will be heard. But what about the money?" "Everything that we talked about before will happen just like I promised. Even what we talked about with your sisters. Hell, the money we will make will put everyone in your family through school if you wanted to. Just trust me, please."

Nathan looks over at Mark and Minty again. Minty turns and walks back into the forest and disappears from site. Mark stays back to see what his friend is going to do. Nathan looks over at Mark and says, "Just think Mark, I could be heard all across the country, maybe even the world."

"Yes, you could. I have told you for a long time your music was good enough for the world."

"So, I think I will go with Robert. I mean it's a once in a lifetime opportunity. I will be the first Negro musician to play in white folks house, ever."

"Nathan, that man cut that rope because you were becoming more popular. He tried to get you killed, and now you are just going to go with him because he promised you fame?"

"No, I think I am going with him because he promised me money."

"But we risked our lives to bring you back home."

"Well, I appreciate you guys doing that, but I didn't ask you too."

Mark looks over at his friend and for the first time doesn't see him the same way as the days of old. His entire facial expression changes and he says to Nathan.

"I went to jail trying to save you. My brother and I risked our lives for you!"

"I'll send you guys some money."

Mark goes to say something to Nathan very aggressively. But as soon as he opens his mouth Robert says from a distance.

"Hey! There is a group of people from the town coming this way, and they don't look happy."

Nathan looks over at Mark, "I better go, and I think you better get out of here too. I will come visit home in a couple of months. By then I will have enough money, and we can forget about all this."

"I think I already have."

Mark looks over Nathan's shoulder to see the light from a torch coming their way. Nathan turns to see what Mark is looking at and sees the same. He turns back around to say goodbye to his friend, and Mark is already gone. Robert yells at Nathan one more time

"Nathan, we have to go!"

Nathan looks for his friend once more before turning and running toward Robert and the carriage. Nathan looks back once more while in the carriage hiding under blankets and instruments to see if he can spot the twins one more time. All he sees, however, are the leaves blowing where Mark once stood.

Minty and the twins return to headquarters where Emmet is waiting for them. He greats Minty with a hug and greeting as she says something to him softly. He then looks over at the twins and says, "So, I guess we have learned a little something."

"Yeah, never risk your life for someone who isn't worth risking it for."

"Yes, and one other thing."

"What is that?"

"In this country when it comes between you and money, you will always be the last option. Ready to go to church?"

"What for?"

"Because I think Walter has something to say to you guys in his sermon. Come on and get dressed."

Emmet directs the boys toward George who is waiting for them with new suits. They get dressed and walk over to the church where there is music playing and people singing. Emmet and the twins walk into a full church. As the boys father prays at the altar, they walkover to him and touch him on the shoulders. He looks up at the sky to thank God for his son's return and stands to his feet in tears and hugs them tightly. The choir sings louder as Elijah walks up to the podium and begins his Sunday sermon.

"Good morning, my people. I want to thank you all for coming this morning, and I want to welcome back some of us who have been away for awhile. I want to talk this morning about the Hebrew Israelite tribe who were lost in the deserts of Africa. This lost tribe of men and women were cursed to roam the lands of Africa for 400 plus years says the bible. And I think we are the dependence of that very tribe. We have been cast out of our own glorious and rich country of Africa to roam the lands of

450

America and try to find a home that is not ours. To be forced to listen and obey laws that weren't made by people that look like us. To turn on each other at a moment's notice for someone that truly doesn't care about what happens to you? Which is really just saying that we are roaming instead of placing a claim on something and making it work. Truth is we have paid for our sins and been slaves on this planet for 400 years. But we will continue to be slaves if we don't pay attention to the way our world works." Truth is, in order to be something in this land you have to own it. Mr. Prescott who lives 20 miles from here, originally moved out there because he didn't get along with the people in the main town. So he started his own town and look at him now, he brings in more cattle to these parts of the area than anyone. I guess the point I am trying to make is when are we going to grow and cultivate our own lands? And not just with the money, but also with spiritual and emotional cultivation. Helping each other with our lands to grow and sell our products fairly amongst ourselves and others. Truthfully, we have harvested and raised this land and its children for a long time now, and I think that it's time we did it more for ourselves than anyone else.

We have to learn how to recognize and eliminate those who are not in our best interest. A man cannot be judged on his skin color, but at the same time realizing that skin color does not give you a pass.

We have to stop blaming the past and what has happened to us in it, for what is happening now. Because the past is just that, a moment in time that affected us in that moment and nothing more. Yes, we have been taught to hate ourselves over the years and for all we know there are more things they will throw at us to continue this rotting from the inside. But, it is up to us to stop the madness that we see as a People on our own. We have to fix the problem no matter where it comes from or how it started.

Because blaming the source does nothing if you look to it for help. Let's work on us and fight for what we want as a People, just like every other race in this country. And maybe then they will stop stepping on us when they realize we stopped stepping on ourselves. Now for those of you that have bibles, I would like you to turn to James chapter 2 verses 14-26, and for those who don't or cannot read I will read it for you.

Elijah waits for a moment as those who have bibles find the scripture he has asked them to go to.

Just as Elijah goes to read the bible verse, one of the people standing in the back of the church leaves and walks out of the town. Elijah looks up at the man as he leaves the church and smiles to himself as if it was something he knew would happen. He leaves the town and runs to Mr. and Mrs. Lesure's home where he is quickly taken upstairs after talking to the man at the door. They both quickly walk up the stairs into the day room where Mr. and Mrs. Lesure are sitting with their guest Congressman Nelson. The man tips his hat to the Lesure's and walks directly over to the Congressman. He whispers something to the Congressman, and his face lights up from the information. He reaches into his pocket and hands the man a large sum of money out of his bill fold. The man acknowledges the Lesure family again without saying a word and quickly walks out of the house room and house.

Mr. Lesure sitting next to his wife says to Congressman Nelson as he gazes into the fireplace, "Must have been important information for you to have given him such a large sum of money. I hope it was worth it."

"It was. It's a part of the reason I am here in the first place. I have been looking for a woman that has eluded the local authorities and even the government for years now. Our research says that she is somewhere close to here, but so far there have been no sightings. But, you have two boys that have been gone for some time now who have returned today, and our sources say she was with them."

"And who is this woman? Maybe we would know her if she lives here."

"She doesn't live here, ma'am. She has been coming to the south for years before slavery was abolished to help slaves escape to the country of Canada. She has been a part of several attempts to help the Negro anyway that she can, she

454

has been successful in some of her journeys but not all. We have found that the people are using her nick name which is Minty, but we know her as Harriet. She has terrorized plantation owners for years by stealing their property and even killing some of them."

"How come this is the first time we are hearing of this? We have heard of a woman by that name, but we have never heard about her killing off innocent white plantation owners."

"Innocent is a strong word, Mr. Lesure. And the reason you have never heard such a story is because we don't want to scare the white folk, and we don't want to give the Negros a sense of hope. Remember the winners in war are the ones who write the story."
"Well, what does that mean?"

Congressman looks over at Mrs. Lesure and says to her, "Mrs. Lesure I want to first thank you for all you have done with me visiting your home. The food and the hospitality have been second-to-none, and it is greatly appreciated."

"You are welcome, Congressman."

"With that being said I want to ask if you would allow your husband and I to have a moment to ourselves? There are some things that need to be addressed privately." Mrs. Lesure looks over at her husband, and Mr. Lesure nods at his wife to do as the Congressman says. She gets up out of her seat and excuses herself as the Congressman closes the door behind her.

"Since the day America decided that slavery was the key to our success we have been studying and researching what makes these people function. Why is it that they are the only race of people that can withstand all elements of weather, strong as a mule, and as wise as an old man? Tell me, Lesure do you believe in God?"

"Of course I do."

"Would you believe me if I told you that the entire bible is correct until we talk about God's son?"

"Why would I believe that?"

"Not in the fact that he existed on earth. But the fact that he was never a white man at all. You know that the story takes place in Jerusalem and cities that still stand in the country of Africa which only produced people that look like the servants you have here in your home. We have known that for centuries, which is why we destroyed the faces of the sphinxes of Egypt. Which is why we commissioned the greatest painter in Leanardo Di Vinci to paint what he thought Jesus looked like. And it is also why now in this country we force it on them to believe, so that maybe if we continue to train their minds, they will never find out the truth."

"The truth?"

Congressman Nelson looks Mr. Lesure directly in the eyes and says softly, "The truth that they are the original man, and have every right to treat us the way we have treated them for centuries. Every other race is a downgrade of God's original design, and it shows in our everyday lives. Which is why we need to control them as much as possible, it's the only way they will never reach their potential in this country. William Lynch came to this country in the 1700's to show is the way of controlling them, and everything that he said worked until now. So, we have to find new ways of keeping them distracted and right now it is money. Everyone wants it, and willing to turn on their own to get it. And the more we encourage it for them while watching from afar, the longer it will take them to correct it which will give us more time to try to eliminate them as a whole. We have found out that Marthasville is the central location of their headquarters and it is up to us stop what they are slowly starting to learn."

"And what is that?"
"The writer of the book is the winner of the war. Just ask the Indians. Let's share in a toast to the wealthy in America."

"Why not the white race?"

"Because race is what keeps people distracted from the fact that they are all poor. And the true-inventors of racism were the rich trying to hold on to what they had acquired."

"What do you mean?"

"My young Senator you have a lot to learn about what this country is about. Cheers!" They both raise their glasses and toast to what the Congressman has said. Mr. Lesure, not sure of what he has just heard, smiles nervously at the Congressman because he knows there is something more to his statement.

Outside of the door, Emmet stands and overhears the conversation and rushes out of the house in order to go back to the lake.

Emmet knows with the new overheard information that the fight is just beginning and the interest of his friend is bigger than he could have imagined. He can only hope that through whatever is coming next that they address it together.